People were crowding around her hospital bed...

And Caroline didn't recognize a soul!

"I thought she was okay," said a man in blue jeans.

Caroline couldn't help but admit her attraction to him—and she liked the anxious look he sent the doctor.

"She is," the doctor returned. "But with the baby..."

Baby? Caroline's hand shot to her stomach. She was pregnant! She couldn't be. Could she? Oh dear, what had she gotten herself into? And with whom?

A look at the shocked faces told her that no one had known.

"I demand to know who the father is!" the eldest man present suddenly shouted.

With that tone, Caroline was pretty sure he was *her* father.

"Who?" he repeated.

Then three men stepped forward. In unison, as if rehearsed, they all said, "I am."

Dear Reader,

We're expecting! American Romance is proud to announce our NEW ARRIVALS subseries. This spring some very special authors are inviting you to read about equally special heroines—all of whom are on a nine-month adventure! We expect each soon-to-be mom will find the man of her dreams— and a daddy in the bargain!

This month delivers: *Who's the Daddy?* by Judy Christenberry.

Our feisty heroine, Caroline Adkins, gets more than she bargains for when she awakens in a hospital bed with amnesia—only to find out she's pregnant! And that there are three different men claiming paternity....

We hope you'll love this adventurous tale of romance—only from American Romance!

Sincerely,

**Debra Matteucci
Senior Editor and Editorial Coordinator
American Romance & Intrigue**

Judy Christenberry

WHO'S THE DADDY?

Harlequin Books

TORONTO • NEW YORK • LONDON
AMSTERDAM • PARIS • SYDNEY • HAMBURG
STOCKHOLM • ATHENS • TOKYO • MILAN
MADRID • WARSAW • BUDAPEST • AUCKLAND

For my mother Faye Russell—

for her support and encouragement through the years

ISBN 0-373-16579-X

WHO'S THE DADDY?

Copyright © 1995 by Judy Christenberry

Chapter One

"Memorial Hospital, on line one."

James Adkins, one of the wealthiest men in Denver, reared back in his chair, ran a hand through his gray hair, slammed his bifocals onto the table and glared at his secretary. "I told you I was not to be disturbed."

"Yes, sir, but it's Caroline. She's in the hospital."

"That girl of mine is always running around getting involved in causes. Tell her we'll discuss it over dinner." He turned away, assurance in every ounce of him that he'd be obeyed. After all, he always was.

"Sir," the secretary persisted, desperation in her voice, "she's there as a patient."

He turned to stare at her, his frown of impatience turning to deeper emotion. "What? That's ridiculous. I saw her this morning."

"There was an accident," the secretary said quickly.

James Adkins moved faster than one would have expected from his less than sleek figure, overweight from rich foods and no exercise. He grabbed the phone and barked into it. "Who's speaking?"

The two men with whom he'd been meeting both stood and moved closer to the phone.

"She's what?" Adkins shrieked, and then listened again. "Yes, yes, I'll be right there! Yes, I'll bring her mother." He slammed down the receiver and looked at the two younger men, for the first time unsure of his actions.

"Caroline's been in an accident. And…and she's got amnesia."

"Is she all right?" one of them asked.

"I just told you she has amnesia!" James snapped.

"But the accident— Is she hurt?"

"No, only bruised. Prescott, go to another phone and tell Lewis to bring the limo around. Adrian, you call Tucker and tell him he'll have to wait on my decision. I've got to call her mother and Chelsea."

As was their custom, the two men jumped to do his bidding. He growled to his secretary, "Find my wife. I believe she's attending the symphony auxiliary this morning. I'll try to reach my younger daughter."

The woman scurried from the room, as if grateful to have escaped.

"Chelsea? This is your father. Are you dressed?"

"Hi, Daddy. No, I'm still resting. Expectant mothers should get lots of rest, you know. Roddy agrees with me."

"I'm coming to pick you up. Your sister's been in an accident. She's not badly hurt, but she's lost her memory. The doctor thinks familiar faces will bring it back."

"But Daddy, why do *I* have to go? Pregnant mothers shouldn't get upset or go to hospitals. They have germs there."

"Chelsea, you have ten minutes to get ready. Don't keep me waiting," he warned in ominous tones.

"Your wife is on line two, sir," the secretary said softly from the door.

James nodded and told his daughter goodbye in the midst of another protest.

"Amelia? Caroline's okay but she's been in an accident."

"Oh, dear. But she's all right?"

He breathed a sigh of relief. Amelia might not be the perfect mother, but she loved her children. "Yes, well, she's lost her memory. It's temporary, of course, but—"

"Her memory? You mean she doesn't remember who she is? That's horrible. Why—why, she might think she's some—some common woman, not—"

"Amelia! We'll be there to pick you up in five minutes."

"Pick me up?" she asked in puzzled tones.

"Yes, the doctor said you should come. It might help Caroline's memory come back."

"But—but I'm in the middle of my meeting. Couldn't I come when I'm free? After all, I'm sure—"

"Five minutes, Amelia. I'll come in and drag you out if you're not waiting."

"James!" Amelia squealed as he hung up the phone.

Damn females! They drove him crazy. First Caroline with her independence, then Amelia with her social life. And he didn't know what to do about Chelsea.

He rushed out the door, hearing his secretary murmur, as he passed her, that the limo was waiting downstairs. Of course it was. The driver was a man and always did exactly what he was supposed to do. It was only females—three particular females—who gave James any difficulty.

When he reached the front door, he found both men who'd been in his office standing in front of the limo arguing.

"What's going on?"

"I think I should come with you, James. After all, Caroline and I have been seeing quite a bit of each other, and I might be able to help," Prescott Brownlee said at once.

"She was with *me* last night, at the opera ball," Adrian Meadows inserted, stepping closer to his boss. "Since we were just together, she might remember me more. Besides, James, you may need some help with details."

"Fine, both of you can come. I want her memory restored as soon as possible. I won't tolerate anything less. She's been acting strange lately. It's time for things to get back to normal around here. You hear me?"

Both men nodded and stood at attention as he got into the limo, neither daring to suggest that some things might be beyond James Adkins's control. They weren't sure *anything* was. Then they quickly scrambled after him, each one trying to enter first.

As the limo pulled out into traffic, James clenched his hands into fists. "If either one of you had convinced Caroline to marry him, she'd be home having a baby, like Chelsea, instead of running around having accidents!"

Both men protested their innocence, each assuring James he'd done everything in his power to court Caroline.

"Last night she really enjoyed herself," Adrian added, shooting a smug look at Prescott. "We danced all evening."

"Did you ask her?"

All three men knew what James was referring to. Adrian met neither of the others' gazes. "No. Uh, the time didn't seem right. But I'm sure she'll accept when I do."

Prescott snorted in derision, a knowing look in his eyes. James ignored both of them. "She'll make up her mind soon. I've sensed a readiness to settle down. We'll get her memory back, and then she'll marry one of you."

Neither of them argued with him. But then they never did.

"COME ON, MAX, give us a break. You've driven the entire crew like they were dogs the past few weeks. And they've done a good job. Let's give them tomorrow off, let'm have a four-day weekend for Labor Day."

Max Daniels pinched the bridge of his nose and closed his eyes briefly. His foreman, Jim Swensen, hadn't lied. He'd been a bear to work for, and he knew it. "Okay. That's a good idea, Jim. Give'm Friday off."

Jim slapped him on his shoulder. "Great. The guys'll be glad to hear it." He paused and Max tensed for what would come next.

"You still don't want to talk about what's buggin' you?"

He offered a brief smile to compensate for his negative answer. "No. But thanks for the offer. I'll see you on Tuesday."

"All right, man, but if you need to talk—"

"I'll know where to find you. Thanks, Jim."

Max watched as his foreman, also his best friend, headed toward the group of workers putting away their tools.

Slamming the truck in reverse, he backed out of the makeshift driveway, wanting to get away before any of the men came over to thank him for the extra holiday.

He knew he didn't deserve their thanks. He'd been impossible to work with for two months. No question. But he couldn't explain to them that he'd fallen in love and been abandoned by the woman with no explanation, no goodbye. One minute, bliss, the next, hell. And he was afraid that he'd demanded company in his personal hell, from everyone around him.

Man, he had to get a grip on himself. He'd never thought a woman would send him into such a tailspin. He still didn't understand why. She was beautiful, but he'd dated women more beautiful. She was intelligent, charming, but no more so than others. Her sense of humor delighted him, making him eager to share the events of his day with her, waiting to hear her warm chuckles. Her kisses—

A blaring horn reminded him the light had turned green and he stepped on the accelerator. Just as well. No sense following that line of thought.

He reached for the radio, seeking distraction. It was five after five and the national news had just ended.

"Now, in local news, Caroline Adkins, daughter of—"

Max almost drove off the road. Horns blared around him and the woman behind him sailed past, shaking an angry fist.

He pulled to a stop, reaching for the volume knob.

"...in an accident. A Memorial Hospital spokesman said she will be kept overnight for observation."

Without considering the consequences, he swung the truck back on the road and did an illegal U-turn at the next intersection. In two minutes, he was pulling into the parking lot at Memorial Hospital.

Please, God, let her be all right.

And if she was, he was going to break her neck for running out on the best thing that had ever happened to him.

"DID CAROLINE ASK to see me?" Amelia asked as the limo pulled into the hospital parking lot.

James sighed with impatience. "I told you, Amelia, she's lost her memory."

"Yes, dear, but if she didn't ask for me, I don't see why I couldn't have come after my meeting ended. Agnes told me I shouldn't always do whatever you say, you know."

James and his second daughter, Chelsea, groaned together. "That woman," James said through gritted teeth, "never agrees with me."

"Well, I know Caro didn't ask to see me," Chelsea said before her mother could respond. Her lips formed into a pout that seemed natural. "She never even calls me. You would think, now that she's to be an aunt, that she would show some interest in my baby.''

"She told me last night how excited she was about your baby," Adrian assured Chelsea hurriedly, as if hoping to stem her complaints.

"Really? Well, she should spend more time with me, then," Chelsea said.

The limo pulled to a stop, and the chauffeur opened the door. All three men hurried out and then turned to help the two women.

"I think we should tell the doctor that I'm pregnant before I go into Caro's room, in case there could be any danger," Chelsea continued as they approached the front doors.

"Amnesia isn't contagious!" James snapped. He'd silently endured the complaints of both women for the length of the ride, but he was anxious for word of Caroline.

He would admit, though not to Amelia and Chelsea, that Caroline was his favorite. Not that they didn't fight. On the contrary, Caroline argued with him at every turn. She was too much like him not to.

Chelsea was like her mother.

"Chelsea!" someone called, and they all halted.

Chelsea's husband, Roderick Grant III, hurried up to them.

"What are you doing here?" James demanded. He didn't have anything against the boy, but Roddy wouldn't be of much help in a crisis.

"Daddy! Roddy's my husband!"

"I know that. I paid for that damned wedding, didn't I?" He muttered an apology when Chelsea and Amelia stared at him in shock. "I'm worried about Caroline," he added.

"Of course, you are, sir," Adrian said, patting him on the shoulder.

"Why don't we go right up," Prescott added. "I'll find out her room number."

"I know it. It's 482," James snapped, and strode for the elevators, leaving his entourage to hurry after him.

When they reached the fourth floor, the nurse on duty ushered all of them into the waiting room. "The doctor is with her now. I'll let you know when you can go in."

"Damn it, woman, I'm James Adkins. You go tell that doctor I want to see my child at once!" As the nurse calmly walked away, he bellowed, "Why won't any woman listen to me?

"CAROLINE ADKINS, where can I find her?" Max had no idea how he'd gotten from the road outside the site to the hospital information desk.

"Is she a patient, sir?" the grandmotherly lady in a pink pinafore asked, smiling benignly at him.

"She was in an accident. They said they're holding her for observation."

"How would you spell that last name?"

Quelling the urge to grab the little old lady by the daintily tied bow at her neck, he spelled Caroline's name.

"She's on the fourth floor. Room 482."

Max was running for the elevator before the lady ever finished talking. After stepping into the first one available, he jammed the close door button after punching the number four.

He'd find Caroline—and this time she wasn't going to get away. Not until he had an explanation.

As soon as he got out of the elevator, he halted a nurse pushing a trolly of trays.

"Which way to 482?" he demanded.

"Just down the hall, sir."

With a hurried thank-you, he followed her direction and spotted the room up ahead of him. He pushed past a small group of people and reached the door.

"Just one minute!"

He looked over his shoulder to see a large man in both height and girth staring at him. "Yes?"

"Where are you going?"

"What business is it of yours?" he demanded.

"That's my daughter's room."

Max checked to see if he had the right room number. He did. "The desk said this was Caroline Adkins's room. I think you've made a mistake." He was sure Caroline didn't have anyone close by, much less a mob of people.

"I don't make mistakes!"

Max shrugged his shoulders and pushed open the door.

The man grabbed his arm before he could take more than a step into the room. "Who are you and why are you visiting my daughter? Are you the one who hit her?"

"I'm not visiting your daughter. I'm visiting Caroline Adkins," Max explained impatiently. "If this isn't her room—"

"Why would we come here if it's not Caroline's room?" Amelia asked plaintively.

"Sir, I think you're making a mistake," a younger man in an elegant business suit said, and Max glared at him. The young lady in the group began complaining about feeling faint. A man quickly supported her, and Max turned back toward the room only to find himself confronted by a man in a white coat.

"What is going on here?" he asked with quiet authority.

"I'm here to visit Caroline Adkins," Max explained.

Immediately behind him, several voices both protested his visit and demanded information about Caroline. What was wrong with these people? Max couldn't figure out why they were there. As far as he knew, Caroline had just moved to the area and had no one nearby.

"Quiet," the doctor commanded. The one word quelled even the older man who'd been protesting his presence, Max noted.

"You may all see Caroline, but she has a headache. Please keep quiet and don't ask her any questions."

Max frowned. He could wait for his questions to be answered, as long as he didn't lose her again. He *couldn't* lose her again.

THE SUDDEN NOISE at the door of her room had increased the pain in her head. The nurse touched her shoulder and smiled, silently encouraging her to relax.

Oh, sure. It was easy for the nurse. She hadn't lost her memory. She knew her name. And if she forgot, it was right there on her name tag.

The doctor had told her her name was Caroline. But there was no sense of recognition, no satisfaction. Just confusion. And, as much as she fought it, panic.

All she knew was what she'd been told since she'd awakened in the hospital. There'd been a wreck, a hit and run, and she'd smacked her head on the windshield even though she'd worn her seat belt. Her purse had been beside her, giving the doctor her name. He said he'd called her family.

If her family was making all the noise, she wasn't sure she wanted to see them. At least not yet.

Suddenly her bed was surrounded by people.

People.

But no one she knew.

She hadn't realized how much she'd hoped she would recognize her family when they arrived until that moment. You'd think she could at least recall her parents. Even though she could identify the two likeliest suspects by their age, her mouth went dry at the blankness that filled her.

Her gaze shifted to the first one who'd entered, seeking a distraction. He was somehow different from the rest of them. Rugged. And very attractive. *I don't know who I am, but at least I know what I like.*

She hurriedly looked away as a horrible thought struck her.

What if he was her brother?

The older man stepped forward and picked up her hand.

"Caroline, are you okay?"

She said faintly, "Yes, I'm fine."

As if he didn't believe her, he looked at the doctor.

"Are you Mr. Adkins?" the doctor asked.

"Yes."

"I'm Dr. Johansen. Your daughter is in good condition, considering the accident."

"Fine, fine. When can I take her home?"

She couldn't help the panicked gaze she sent to the doctor. These people were all strangers. She didn't want to go with them.

Before the doctor could answer, the older lady pushed through the crowd to the side of the bed. "You're fine, aren't you, Caroline? I know you wouldn't have asked me to leave my meeting. I told your father that, and Agnes agreed."

The younger woman groaned. "Mother, do you have to repeat everything Agnes says? Besides, I'm the one who shouldn't have come. After all, I'm expecting."

Caroline frowned. The young lady announced her condition as if she were the first pregnant woman in the world. As her lips quirked slightly, Caroline discovered something new about herself. She had a sense of humor. *Thank goodness. I'd hate to live with these people and not know how to laugh.*

She looked at the four men who hadn't spoken. Three of them were in expensive business suits. The other man, the one who'd first caught her attention, was dressed in jeans and a short sleeved shirt. He was slightly taller than the others, and his muscled figure was bronzed from the sun.

He opened his mouth, as if to speak, when the doctor said, "I understand how much you'd like to take her home at once, but, in her condition, I think we should keep her overnight for observation."

"I thought you said she was okay," the man in blue jeans snapped. Caroline liked the anxious look he sent the doctor.

"She is. But with the baby—"

"Oh, that's all right. I don't live at home anymore. She won't bother me," the young woman told the doctor with a superior air. "My husband and I have our own home, quite lovely, just a few blocks away from Daddy."

Dr. Johansen looked nonplussed, the first time he'd been stumped since Caroline met him after she'd awakened. Finally he said, "I think you misunderstood me. I wasn't referring to your baby, young lady, but Caroline's. She's pregnant."

In the silence that followed his explanation, Caroline moved her hand to her stomach, unable to believe the doctor's words. Pregnant? She couldn't be. Could she? Oh, dear, what had she gotten herself into?

And with whom?

A look at the shocked faces around her told her that no one else had known.

Then the young woman whimpered. "I should've known. I should've known you'd go out and get pregnant just to spite me. You always think you have to be better than me!" She broke into sobs, burying her face in the suit jacket of one of the younger men.

"Oh, no, dear, no. This is all my fault," said the woman she supposed was her mother.

The man who claimed to be her father turned to stare at the woman. "What are you talking about, Amelia?"

Amelia? Her mother's name was Amelia?

"I should never have asked Caroline to work in the unwed mother's home. It's my fault."

"Amelia, pregnancy isn't contagious, either!" the man ranted, his face turning red.

Caroline almost felt sorry for him. He seemed surrounded by some very strange people.

Dr. Johansen spoke again. "I apologize. I didn't realize you didn't know about the pregnancy. Of course, she's only two months along, but usually—"

"Two months?" Mr. Blue Jeans asked sharply.

"Yes, but—"

"I demand to know who the father is," the older man suddenly exclaimed, glaring at everyone in the room. In that tone of voice, Caroline was sure he was always obeyed.

She was right.

Three men stepped forward, each of them staring at her, and, in unison, as if rehearsed, said, "I am."

Chapter Two

She was sleeping with three men? At the same time? What kind of woman was she?

Caroline stared at each of those who'd claimed parentage to her child. No flicker of recognition arose. She was debating what her response should be when everyone else in the room spoke for her.

"I don't understand," Amelia said, a puzzled look on her brow.

"Well, I do! Caroline, how disgusting," her sister said, staring down her nose at Caroline.

"That's impossible!" James Adkins roared. "You couldn't be the father of her child!"

Caroline frowned as she realized her father was only speaking to the odd man out, the one in blue jeans. Her father didn't have a problem with the other two men claiming to be the father of her child? What qualified them? The fact that they were wearing suits?

After directing a glare at her father, the man turned to look at Caroline. She found herself swallowed up by his burning gaze.

"Oh, yes, I certainly could," he said, with no doubt in his voice.

If it were a matter of attraction, she'd accept his word, hands down, she realized. But it wasn't. "Who are you?" she asked.

There was a flash of disappointment in his gaze, but it disappeared almost at once. "Max Daniels."

"We—we dated?"

"Briefly."

"Caroline, the man is obviously after your money. I'll get rid of him," James Adkins promised, ar l then motioned to the other two daddy candidates.

She didn't know who she was, or who these people were, but she did know she didn't take kindly to being overruled. "I don't think that decision is yours to make."

The uproar her assertion of independence brought from her father, the other two men, even her mother and sister, was enough to make Caroline's headache feel like a volcanic eruption.

Even in pain, however, she noticed that the center of the controversy, Mr. Blue Jeans, shot her a look of approval. Well, he needn't think he was home free. She wasn't about to take a stranger's word about such an important matter.

She was struck by the irony of calling the man a stranger when he might be the father of her child.

"I asked you not to question or upset her," Dr. Johansen interrupted. "You'll all have to leave now."

Though they didn't go quietly, the doctor herded the visitors from the room and left Caroline in peace.

As much peace as one could have, pregnant without knowing who the father might be.

Could she really have been sleeping with three men? Was she the kind of woman who hopped from bed to bed? Revulsion filled her and she wanted to believe that was not possible. But then why were three men claiming to be the daddy?

She recalled her father's remark, that Max Daniels was only after her money. Once the pregnancy had been revealed, she hadn't thought about her life before the accident. She was wealthy? Not that she objected. Not having to worry about paying hospital bills would be an advantage.

But she needed answers! She wanted to reclaim her life, to understand what was happening to her. And most of all, she wanted to know which man had made love to her two months ago. And heaven help her if it was more than one.

"ARE YOU ALL PACKED?" the nurse asked cheerfully, coming into her room the next morning.

Caroline murmured yes, not bothering to point out she had almost nothing to pack. She didn't move her head, however. Even after twenty-four hours, it felt fragile. "Is—is my father here?"

She still wasn't comfortable with James Adkins, or the other members of her family. Or even with herself, for that matter. She'd looked in a mirror and seen a stranger. A pregnant stranger.

That thought had been brought home to her when she'd gotten up this morning. Morning sickness, heightened by her concussion, the nurse had said, had attacked her. What little breakfast she'd eaten had come right back up.

Women go through this more than once? Voluntarily? The nurse had reassured her that her sickness was perfectly normal in the circumstances.

"He called earlier to let us know he was picking you up at ten. It's almost that now. I'll bring a cart for the flowers."

Her father had flooded her room with floral arrangements. Even more interesting had been the offerings from two of the men claiming to have fathered her baby. Long-stemmed red roses. Two dozen apiece.

Nothing from Max Daniels.

"Why don't you pass the flowers out among the sick?" Caroline said. "I think that might be easier than carting them all home." *Wherever that was.*

"That's very generous of you. I have several patients who never receive flowers." The nurse smiled.

"Then I hope they enjoy these."

Footsteps near the door had her turning around carefully. But it was neither the doctor nor her father. Her heartbeat picked up speed as she stared at Max Daniels.

How could she have forgotten making love to this man? He was certainly handsome, but there was something more—a connection she couldn't explain—that took her breath away. She noted he was again in jeans, this time coupled with a starched plaid shirt, and he held a bouquet of daisies in his hand.

"Good morning," he said.

She responded and waited, watching him. His eyes, as blue as the sky, looked wary, as if he weren't sure of his welcome. The nurse slipped from the room, murmuring something about fetching a cart. Left alone with him, Caroline's mouth went dry as she stared at the gorgeous man in front of her. The urge to touch him almost consumed her. When Max continued to say nothing, she asked in desperation, "Are those for me?"

He held the flowers out to her. "Yeah." His gaze took in the roses and carnations that filled the room. "You told me you liked daisies."

If she hadn't before, she did now. If Max Daniels delivered them. "I do, thank you. That's very thoughtful of you."

"Has your memory returned?" He took a step closer, his gaze intent.

She started to shake her head and then stopped. The headache hovering on the edge of consciousness edged closer with any radical movement. "No, it hasn't."

He thrust the flowers into her hands and stepped back. "Then how can I get a phone number where I can reach you? I'd like to stay in touch."

"You don't have it?" *Some relationship they must've had. If he was telling the truth.*

"No. If I'd had it, I would've found you a lot sooner," he said gruffly, a fierceness entering his gaze that had her stepping back.

Either the movement, or the puzzle that was her life at the moment, pushed the headache out of control. She reached for her forehead with her free hand, clasping the daisies to her breast with the other.

"Are you all right?"

"I need to sit down," she said faintly, and he guided her to the only chair. As she was sinking into it, her head lolling back against the top of it, the door to her room was pushed open.

"What are you doing to my daughter?" a booming voice demanded.

Caroline dropped the flowers into her lap and pressed both hands to her throbbing temples. "Please—"

Without answering her father's question, Max walked to the bed and pressed the nurse's button.

"I'm sorry, Caro, I didn't mean to make your head hurt," James Adkins hurriedly apologized, and then glared at Max, as if it were Max's fault he had yelled.

"Yes?" the nurse asked as she came back into the room.

"Ms. Adkins's headache has come back," Max said softly. "Is there anything you can give her for it?"

"It never went away," Caroline contradicted him.

"Because of the baby, we can't give her a painkiller. She just needs to have peace and quiet." The nurse glared accusingly at the two men.

"I'm here to take her home," her father said stiffly. "I don't know why *he's* here."

"Well, she needs to be back in bed as soon as possible. The doctor's on the way up to release her." She backed out of the room, still frowning at Caroline's visitors.

"He wants my phone number," Caroline told her father. "Would you give it to him, please? I don't remember it. And get his." Stupid statement. No one would expect her to remember a phone number when she couldn't even remember her shoe size.

But she didn't want to lose Max Daniels. Her reaction to him told her he had to be the one—the father of

her baby. The love of her life? Frustration filled her—
and not a little panic. What if she never remembered?
What if—

Her father disrupted her fears by glaring at Max
again and moving closer to her chair to say in a stage
whisper obviously intended for Max's ears, "Caroline,
I'm not sure that's wise. We only have his say-so that
you two were—you know."

Caroline rolled her eyes. Great. Next her father would
want to explain the birds and the bees. "Intimate.
That's the word. Please give him my phone number."

Max stepped forward, ignoring her father, and extended a business card to her. "Both my work and home
numbers are on this card. Call me if there's anything I
can do for you—or anything."

"You've already done too much, according to you!"
her father growled.

Max's lips—those enticing lips—flattened tightly
against each other, and Caroline had the strangest urge
to tease them into a smile. As attracted as she was to
Max Daniels, if he was the father of her child, she felt
sure she had put up no resistance whatsoever to any intimacy between them. In fact, *she* may have seduced
him.

But what about the other two men who claimed to be
the daddy? She wished she could rule them out, but she
reluctantly admitted she couldn't. She'd read about
women who carried on with more than one man, but—
she had?

Distracted by a memory, even an insignificant one,
she lost track of the men's conversation. It was such a

relief to remember something, even though it was useless for solving her problems.

"Look, Mr. Adkins," Max said, moving closer to the older man, "what happened is between Caroline and me. What's her phone number?"

"It's unlisted."

"I figured that. I called all the Adkinses as I could find in the telephone book."

That remark snapped her from her thoughts. "You did?"

"You disappeared without saying goodbye. I wanted to know why." His expression said he blamed her for her unexplained departure.

She'd like to know why she'd gone away, too. Why would she leave someone she was obviously attracted to? Had she found out some deep, dark secret? Or was his entire story a lie?

"She probably realized she was in love with Prescott or Adrian. She came back to them, didn't she?" James offered.

Her father's interpretation of past events might not be quite reliable, Caroline decided. He seemed intent on persuading her that one of the other men was the mysterious father.

"By the way, where *are* the Bobbsey twins?" she asked.

Max choked and tried to hide a chuckle behind one of his big hands. Her gaze remained fixed on his crinkling blue eyes, hoping for a glimpse of his smile.

"Caroline! You shouldn't call them such a thing. They're down in the limo, waiting. They wanted to

come up here, but I assured them we'd be right down."
James glared at Max again.

"They really came?" She'd only been teasing, hoping to lighten the moment.

"Of course. They're very concerned about you." He
waved to the roses on each side of her bed. "After all,
they sent you roses, a lot more expensive than those
daisies."

In spite of her headache, Caroline smelled a rat and
asked, "How do you know the roses came from them?"

"Well, I thought— I suggested— It was just a guess."
He blundered to a stop.

As if it were a natural occurrence, her gaze flew to
Max's and they shared a smile, a glorious smile that
she'd been waiting to see. She took a deep breath of
appreciation. The guy was as sexy as could be. She
wondered what he'd look like without his shirt.

"Caroline!" Her father was obviously irritated at her
distraction.

"Please, my head."

Both the doctor and the nurse returned to her room
at that moment, the nurse pushing a flower cart.

"All ready to go, Caroline?" Dr. Johansen asked
cheerfully.

"Yes, I guess so. But my headache is getting worse
again."

"Hmm. Probably the excitement of getting out of
here. I don't know why people react to hospitals that
way," he teased as he picked up her wrist to take her
pulse.

The door opened again to admit the two men her father called Adrian and Prescott. "James? We thought

we'd better come up in case you needed help," Prescott said, his gaze sweeping the room. When it landed on Max, he stepped closer to James.

Interesting, Caroline decided. *He goes to my father's side, not mine.* Adrian, the second one, kind of hovered between her father and her, as if undecided about where his loyalties lay. As they moved, Caroline looked closely at them. They were both handsome, in a conventional manner. Adrian was blond, but a little too smooth for her tastes. Prescott was darker and slightly shorter, but neither stirred her as Max did.

"What's *he* doing here?" Prescott demanded, disdainfully waving his hand toward Max.

"He never left," Caroline rapidly answered, not happy with Prescott's attitude. What business was it of his if Max wanted to visit her? "We spent the entire night together."

Everyone except Max and the doctor gasped, staring at her. Then a babble of protests made her regret her short-tempered response. "Just kidding, just kidding," she said, raising her hand to halt their noise.

"Caroline's headache is back. Too much noise is bad for it," Max said calmly.

Prescott glared at Max, but Adrian moved closer to Caroline. "Is there anything I can do?"

"Yes. Do you know my phone number?" she asked.

"Why, certainly. Your private line or your father's?"

"Mine."

He said her telephone number, and Caroline smiled as Max took a pen from his shirt pocket and wrote it down on one of his business cards. His sexy grin was her thank-you.

"I'm not sure that was wise, Caroline," Prescott said, echoing her father's earlier warning.

"I may not remember too much about my past, but I know I don't like people bossing me around, whoever I am. If you know me well, Prescott, you must already be aware of that trait."

During their conversation, the nurse had pushed the flower cart out the door and returned with a wheelchair. "Is she ready, Doctor?"

"I believe she is. She may not be up to full fighting weight just yet, but I think she can handle this crew," Dr. Johansen said with a smile at Caroline. "I suspect you've already seen a doctor about your pregnancy, but if not, set up an appointment as soon as possible. And let me know if the headache doesn't gradually diminish."

"Gradually?" she protested.

"I'm afraid so, Caroline. Don't get too agitated for a while. Rest and sleep. That's the cure."

"Thank you, Doctor."

He excused himself and the nurse pushed the wheelchair to her side and then took her arm. "Okay, lean on me. On the count of three, we'll move to the chair."

Caroline would have preferred Max's help, but if she asked for it, Prescott would probably knock both of them over trying to reach her first. She stood and stepped over to the wheelchair. A sudden hand on her other arm needed no identification. The responsive surge of attraction told her it was Max. She smiled up at him once she was settled. "Thanks."

"I would've helped. You should've asked me," Prescott complained.

She almost groaned aloud. If Prescott was the father of her baby, she could expect a whiner and probably the biggest brownnoser in existence. What a depressing thought.

"Well, let's be on our way," her father said abruptly, swinging around to the door. His two satellites fell into step behind him.

Caroline wasn't quite ready. She wanted an excuse to touch Max one more time. Reaching out her hand, she said, "Thank you for the daisies."

He took her hand in his. "My pleasure." Then he leaned down and briefly caressed her lips with his. Her pulse throbbed. Good thing she was going to get some rest before she saw him again. Otherwise, she just might explode with all the excitement.

As if realizing something had occurred behind their backs, the other three men turned and stared at the two of them.

"Are you coming, Caroline?" James demanded.

"Yes, I'm right behind you, Dad," she answered, a smile on her face for Max Daniels. He remained in the room as the nurse pushed her out, her daisies clutched to her chest.

DAMN. Max stood alone in the hospital room and drew a deep breath. He shouldn't have kissed her. But he hadn't been able to resist. Even as pale as she was this morning, with a bruise on her forehead, Caroline was beautiful.

He'd only had two short weeks with her, but he'd missed her every day since she'd gone. Even though he called himself all kinds of a fool for still wanting her.

The two weeks they'd spent together seemed like a dream now, with a nightmare ending when she disappeared. He'd already been making plans for their future together. Plans that were aborted when she left.

She'd told him she was from Kansas City and had just moved to Denver. At first, she'd said she was looking for a job. He'd offered to introduce her to the interior design firms he used, had even told her who to contact. It wasn't until after she left that he realized she'd never looked for a job.

Hell, he hadn't given her time. He'd spent every moment he could with her. He couldn't leave her alone. And he'd been making plans to keep her with him forever.

And now that he'd discovered she was an heiress, he knew they had no future together. Even if the baby was his. Her father wasn't going to let her marry him. Not when there were two superstar executives waiting with open arms.

Max wasn't even sure why he still wanted her. After all, everything she'd told him was a lie. Now he understood the old saying, ignorance is bliss. Those two weeks had certainly been blissful.

But if their two weeks had resulted in a baby, his baby, then he refused to be pushed out of the picture. He would not abandon his own child.

He shook himself from his misery. Feeling sorry for himself had never been his style. Instead, he formulated a plan and set about changing his circumstances.

Maybe that was what had frustrated him so about Caroline. He'd followed every lead he'd had, but he'd discovered nothing about her.

He reached the outer door of the hospital just in time to see a white limo pull away from the hospital. At least this time he had her telephone number. Now all he had to do was come up with a plan.

"WAIT!" PRESCOTT CALLED to the driver as they pulled out of the hospital parking lot.

Caroline rubbed her forehead. "Please don't shout."

"But we've forgotten your flowers. That damned nurse probably thought she could get away with stealing them. Turn around and go back."

"No!" Caroline contradicted. "Take us home, Lewis."

The chauffeur, much to Caroline's satisfaction, obeyed her.

"Caroline!" her father exclaimed. "How did you know?"

"What?" Her head hurt so much. She wasn't sure she could remain upright until they reached the house.

"His name. You knew his name."

"You must have said it," she replied, frowning, trying to think.

"No, I didn't. Your memory is returning!" he exclaimed happily. "That's wonderful. I'll give that doctor a bonus. Now," he said, pausing to lean toward her, "which of these gentlemen is the father of your baby?"

Immediately the headache increased.

"I haven't gotten my memory back. I don't know how I knew his name." She leaned her head back against the seat and closed her eyes. "I'm in so much pain."

"And I don't understand about the flowers. Didn't you like them?" Prescott grumbled.

"They were lovely. But there were so many of them I asked the nurse to distribute them to others who weren't going home. It seemed like the generous thing to do."

"It was, and just like you, Caroline," Adrian said as he smiled at her.

"Was it?" she asked coolly, leery of his friendliness. She decided his gray eyes were cold, even if his lips were smiling. And who knew if he was telling the truth? All she knew about herself so far was that she liked her own way, hated headaches, was pregnant, and apparently didn't mind sleeping with more than one man.

That couldn't be true. She never liked to share. In high school, her boyfriend had thought he could date her and her best friend at the same time. She'd shown him.

Another memory. She clutched it to her like a precious jewel. But when she tried to extend that grasp on the past, searching for other memories, she drew a blank. Frustration filled her.

"If you were so generous with the roses, why are you still holding those?" Prescott complained, gesturing to the daisies.

"Because I like them."

He turned to glare at her father. "You said roses!" he accused. He sounded like a little boy, but his thinning hair showed him to be considerably beyond his youth.

If she'd needed confirmation that the roses had been sent at her father's behest, his remark was it. She shot her father a knowing look.

"I was just trying to speed things up. I don't want my grandchild born a bastard, so I suggest you select one of these fine gentlemen to marry you. They're both willing."

"And are you going to speak the words for them as they mime a proposal?" she asked, growing tired of her father's arguments.

"That's not necessary, Caroline, darling," Prescott said, rushing in, as she should've known he would. She might not remember him, but she knew more about him than she wanted to already.

"I'm perfectly willing to marry you today if you'll agree," he continued, reaching for her hand.

She pulled her hands back. "No, thank you. I have a headache."

Not an original excuse…for a lot of things, but it was the best she could come up with right now.

"I'd prefer to make my proposal in private," Adrian informed her, sending a superior smile toward Prescott.

She'd prefer that he not make it at all. "Thank you, but I'm confused right now. I don't think I'm ready to make any decisions."

"Of course, but you won't forget?" There was an edge to his voice that irritated her.

"I hope not." It seemed to Caroline that a promise not to forget from an amnesiac victim wouldn't be worth much. *She* wouldn't believe her.

"Of course she won't forget," her father answered heartily. "And if she does, the three of us will be there to remind her. After all, she has to marry someone."

"No, I don't."

"Now, Caroline, no argument. I'm an old-fashioned man, and I expect my grandchild to be born on the right side of the blanket."

She ignored him.

"And if you don't cooperate, you just might find yourself written out of my will."

She might not have her memory, but the ease with which her father uttered those words made her suspect it was a threat he'd used before.

"Then call your lawyer, because *I* will decide what I do about *my* baby and *my* future. Not you."

The look of panic on Prescott's face that she might be written out of the will told Caroline her threat may have eliminated at least one potential daddy candidate. Whether her memory returned or not.

Chapter Three

Caroline stared in awe at the magnificent residence the limo stopped in front of, after having driven through a large gate flanked by brick walls. It must take an army of workers to maintain the lush grounds, she decided, her gaze traveling over the perfect flower beds, the exactly trimmed hedges.

She turned to compliment her father on the beauty of their home only to discover everyone staring at her. She felt like a bug under a microscope.

"No, I don't remember," she assured them dryly. "I'll let you know when my memory returns."

All three looked away.

"Why did Prescott and Adrian come with you to pick me up instead of my mother?" Caroline suddenly asked, struck by the presence of these men rather than family members.

"Friday is Save the Whales day," her father muttered.

"I beg your pardon?"

Adrian leaned forward to explain. "Your mother is quite involved in the local charities. On Fridays, she goes to the meeting for saving the whales."

Caroline remembered a curious remark from the day before. "And one of her charities is for unwed mothers?"

"Yes," her father snapped.

Caroline asked no more questions. Not yet.

Her father escorted her into the house and introduced her to the housekeeper, Mrs. Lamb, and then left for the office, accompanied by Prescott and Adrian.

"Welcome home, Caroline. Are you feeling all right?"

"I'm still a little shaky. If you'll show me to my room, I'll lie down for a while."

"Why, honey, there's no need to be formal!" the woman said with a laugh that sent a shooting pain through Caroline's head. "You know better'n me where your room is."

Her patience was wearing thin. Amnesia might play a large role in a lot of jokes, but she wasn't finding it funny. "Mrs. Lamb, I have amnesia. I don't remember ever seeing this house before."

"Oh, my stars. Of course, Caroline. You just come this way. Anything you want to know, you just ask me."

If her head weren't splitting into a chasm the size of the Grand Canyon, she might have taken the woman up on the offer. Later. She only had one question at the moment.

"If I want to invite someone to dinner, is that all right?"

"Of course it is. Just tell me when and how many."

Caroline took a deep breath before she clarified her request. "I meant if I wanted to have a guest for dinner and—and not dine with the family."

"Oh, of course, you want something romanticlike? No problem. It's nice out at night right now. I could set up a table for two on the patio. You'd be all alone there."

"That would be perfect. Thank you, Mrs. Lamb. I'll let you know when."

"Sure enough. I'm just having a little trouble with you being so formal and all. When you wanted something real special from me, you always used to call me Lambie." The woman smiled with a warmth that struck Caroline as the kindest she'd seen since she awoke a lost person.

She reached out and touched Mrs. Lamb's arm. "I'm sorry. I'm sure I'll remember everything soon. If you'll just be patient."

"Of course I will. I'm just glad you weren't hurt bad."

"Thank you."

She followed the housekeeper up a wide staircase, down a long hall to the last door on the right.

"Your room looks out over the pool."

She pushed open the door and Caroline stepped into the room. She stared around her, her eyes wide. "Who decorated it?"

"Why, you did, Caroline, about two years ago. You don't remember? Oh, my stars, what a silly question. Forgive me, child. Now look, here's the phone and if you want anything, you just pick it up and press this button. Okay? I'll be in the kitchen." With a flush of embarrassment on her cheeks, Mrs. Lamb fled the room.

Though she moved about the room, searching for clues to who Caroline Adkins might be, she also recognized a sense of contentment gradually filling her. It felt as if she had finally found a sanctuary from the maze her life had become.

Maybe it's all the blue. I've always been partial to blue. She had taken several more steps before she realized she'd remembered something else about herself. Yes, she'd always liked blues. And bright colors.

With a sigh she pulled back the coverlet on the king-size bed and sank down amid a huge collection of pillows. She'd worry about who she was, what she'd done, later. Now, she needed to rest her aching head.

Caroline awoke several hours later, consciousness gradually returning. But not her memory. She let her gaze sweep the room, looking for clues to who she really was. With a sigh, she sat up.

The rest had given her the energy to indulge her curiosity a little more. After washing her face in the luxurious connecting bath, she returned to the bedroom and opened the closet door.

A ripple of pleasure ran through her as she examined the rows of clothes hung neatly in the large closet. *My, I have great taste...and expensive, too.* She recognized designer names on many of the dresses.

Since she couldn't remember buying or wearing any of the outfits, it was like having an entire new wardrobe. She wouldn't have to shop for months.

Wrong.

How could she forget the baby?

And the changes that would occur in the next few months. She groaned. Even the clothes she was wearing were a little snug, uncomfortably so. Before too long, they wouldn't fit her at all, and she'd have to start shopping all over again.

Not necessarily an unhappy thought, she realized with a grin. What woman didn't enjoy a little shopping? Sliding her hands into the pockets of her navy slacks, she felt the card Max Daniels had given her.

Resolution filled her. She had something more important than shopping to do right now. It was time to take back her life. And she would start with Max Daniels. She ignored the thought that she was starting with him because she *wanted him* to be the father of her child. She had to start somewhere.

She crossed the room to the telephone.

"Daniels Vacation Homes."

Caroline frowned at the sexy female voice that answered the phone. "I'm calling Max Daniels."

"Max is out of the office at the moment. May I take a message?"

"This is Caroline Adkins. I need to—"

"He just came in. One moment, please."

"Caroline?"

She released a sigh at the sound of his voice. It was as if she'd feared she wouldn't find him again. With no memory to support their relationship, she only had those few minutes at the hospital.

"Hi, Max. I—I wanted to invite you to dinner."

The silence that followed her request left a hollow feeling in her stomach.

"To dinner?" he finally asked.

"Yes." When he said nothing else, she asked, "Is that an odd request? Do you not eat?"

"Of course I eat, but you never even admitted you had family in the area, much less offered to introduce me." There was an antagonism in his voice.

"Look, I don't remember what I did...or why. I'm just trying to figure out what happened. I thought I'd start with you. If you don't want to talk to me, then say so." She could match his reluctance any day, she assured herself. Especially if she didn't think about him.

"Of course I want to talk to you. I want to know what happened as much as you do. And whether the baby is mine."

The doubt in his voice was like a blow. "You sounded a lot surer of that fact yesterday."

"That's before I realized I was one of a crowd."

E███████ger filled her, it was tempered by understanding. "It came as a shock to me, too." When he said nothing else, she asked, "Did I ever mention anyone else?"

"No. Like I said, I thought you had recently moved here. That you knew no one."

This discussion was going nowhere. She returned to her original question. "Will you come to dinner? I need to ask you a lot of questions." She didn't intend to plead, but she recognized a hint of persuasiveness in her voice.

"Tell me when."

"Tonight?"

"I can't. I've already made an appointment with prospective clients."

He could've sounded a *little* unhappy that he couldn't come right away. "Tomorrow night?"

Letting out a gusty sigh, he agreed. "What time?"

"Seven o'clock. And would you mind not sounding so put upon? I have no intention of torturing you!" she snapped, any patience she might normally have had having disintegrated between her headache and her heartache.

"It's too late. You already have." He hung up without waiting for a response.

"Oh yeah?" she yelled into the dead phone. "Well, just wait until tomorrow night!"

How dare that man act as if she'd intentionally hurt him? She was suffering just as much as him.

Recalling her bout with morning sickness, she decided she was suffering more. She strode to the closet and her wonderful new wardrobe. He thought he'd been tortured before? She'd make sure the torture continued.

"Caroline?" Mrs. Lamb called softly, rapping on the door before opening it. "Oh!" she exclaimed as Caroline appeared at the closet door.

"Hi. Did you need something?"

"I have a luncheon tray for you," the housekeeper explained, pushing the door open and stepping inside.

"I could've come downstairs," Caroline assured her.

"You're always so thoughtful, child, but you need your rest. What are you doing out of bed?"

"Trying to decide which outfit is my most killer one."

"Killer?" Mrs. Lamb's face was a perfect picture of puzzlement.

"Don't worry. I'm not plotting a murder. I don't think. I'm wanting to, uh, look my best. By the way, my dinner guest is coming tomorrow night. Is that okay?"

"Sure is. Do I know him?"

"His name is Max Daniels." Caroline studied the housekeeper's expression, but she saw no sign of recognition. "You've never heard of him?"

"No. Should I have?"

"He's one of the three . . . Has anyone told you I'm pregnant?"

Mrs. Lamb almost dropped the tray and Caroline rushed forward to support her.

"Oh, my stars. Are you serious? I can't believe it. Isn't that wonderful? You and Chelsea will have babies almost the same age. I—who's the father?"

Mrs. Lamb's abrupt question showed her sudden awareness of Caroline's situation. With a self-conscious shrug, Caroline said, "I don't know. The amnesia."

"Well, surely he'll come forward. I mean, a man should be responsible for his actions."

"That's the problem," Caroline replied. "Three men have claimed responsibility for—for my baby."

"Three? Oh, my stars! Caroline!"

Taking the shaking tray from the housekeeper's hands, Caroline set it on the lamp table. "Lambie, I need help."

"Why, I'll do whatever I—I don't see how—I mean, what are you going to do?"

"I need to find out what was going on in my life two months ago."

As if her knees had collapsed, Mrs. Lamb sank onto the bed. "Oh, my stars."

"What's the matter?"

"Two months ago? A little over two months ago, you had a fight with your father."

"A fight? What about?"

"I don't know. But the next morning, you called a taxi, and you left."

"A taxi? I don't have a car?"

"Of course you have a car. A Mercedes. Your father insisted, saying they were the safest. He buys you a new one every year."

She kept her feelings about her father's domination to herself. "Then why a taxi?"

"I don't know. You had a bag packed and you hugged me, saying not to worry, you were going on a vacation."

"Did I tell you where I was going?"

"No. You left a note for your father, but it didn't tell him anything, 'cause he questioned me."

She had some questions for her father the next time she saw him, too. "Did I call you after I left? And how long was I gone?"

"You called once and told me you were having a good time. And you left a message for your father."

"What message?"

Mrs. Lamb screwed up her face, as if trying to remember, and finally said, "You said you were proving him wrong."

Caroline stared at her. "That's it? Nothing for my mother?"

With a surprised look on her face, Mrs. Lamb said, "Why, no. You don't—I mean, you love your mother, of course, but Mrs. Adkins is so busy..." She trailed off and looked away.

"I see. And when I came back? Did I ever say where I'd been or what I'd done?"

"No. But you seemed sad. Once I found you crying, and that's unusual for you. Why, as a little girl, you'd fall and hurt yourself, but you'd never cry. Unlike Chelsea. Chelsea learned to shed tears whenever she wanted something. Tears just drive your father up the wall."

Caroline could believe that. But she wanted more information about herself, not her father or her sister. "Did I explain why I was crying?"

"No."

"Did I receive any strange phone calls? Or letters?" But she remembered Max asking for her telephone number. He wouldn't have called her.

"No."

"Did I date anyone after I came back?"

"You would go to social events with Adrian and Prescott. You did that before you left, too."

"Social events?"

"You know, to the Save the Whales dinner and dance, the opera, the symphony opening night. There was a real nice picture in the paper yesterday of you and Adrian."

"Why?" Caroline demanded, suddenly afraid she might have announced her engagement.

"You were dancing at the opera ball."

Caroline sat down beside Mrs. Lamb, feeling a little weak herself. And her head was beginning to ache. Again.

Chapter Four

The first dress had to be replaced when she discovered it was too tight.

Fortunately, she made another discovery—an emerald green silk dress, with a V neckline that dipped dangerously low. The flowing skirt ended right at the knees and fluttered every time she moved. If he was a leg man, she'd definitely get his attention.

Max Daniels may have thought she'd tortured him before, but he hadn't seen anything yet.

After perfecting her makeup, she ran downstairs and poked her head through the kitchen door. "Everything okay?"

Mrs. Lamb, working at the huge sink, smiled distractedly. "Oh, yes."

"Thanks. I'll get the doorbell when it rings."

She didn't have long to wait.

Speeding to the front door, she threw it open, a welcoming smile on her face. It faltered when she discovered not one handsome man, but three, on the doorstep.

And none of them looked happy.

"Uh, come in," she muttered, stepping back.

"You'd better eat some lunch, child. You don't look too well. And you've got a baby to think about now."

Caroline smiled faintly. It was too easy to forget that she was carrying a child inside her, since she couldn't remember the event that had brought it about. But Mrs. Lamb was right. She needed to eat.

"Let's take the tray back downstairs. I've had enough eating in bed to last me awhile."

And she needed to calm down again before she faced her father. He had some explaining to do.

SHE DIDN'T GET TO ASK her father any questions that night. Long before he'd returned from the office, she'd gone to bed, exhausted. Her mother had gotten home around four, but her vagueness made Caroline wonder if she even remembered that her daughter had come home from the hospital that day.

Even so, Caroline tried to question her at the dinner table that evening.

"Uh, Mother?"

"Yes, dear?" Amelia replied distractedly, examining the salad she was eating.

"Do you know why I argued with my father?"

"Did you? I have no idea, dear. You argue with him frequently, even though I tell you you shouldn't." She took a bite of salad and chewed it consideringly. "I don't think Mrs. Lamb is using a dietetic dressing, even though I asked her to."

"Please think, Mother. It's important."

"I know it is. I gained two pounds last month, and I'm sure it's the salad dressing."

"No, I mean arguing with—with my father." She had no idea what she normally called him.

Amelia looked at her blankly. "About what? Was he difficult when he picked you up?"

"No, not today," Caroline said, hoping her patience could withstand more conversation with her mother. "Mrs. Lamb said that I had a fight with him a little over two months ago, and then I left."

"Did you? Where did you go?"

Caroline sighed. "I don't know. Didn't you notice I was gone?"

"Hmm. Two months ago? I think that's when I went to that spa in Arizona." She laid down her fork and rang the dinner bell that rested on the table by her plate.

Mrs. Lamb opened the door that led to the kitchen. "Yes, ma'am?"

"Mrs. Lamb, didn't I go to that spa at the end of June?" Amelia asked.

"Was that when I left, while Mother was at the spa?" Caroline added, hoping to clarify matters.

"That's right. Your mother left the day before you did."

"Where did Caroline go, Mrs. Lamb? She wants to know."

The housekeeper looked at Caroline and then her mother. "I don't know, ma'am. She didn't say."

"Thank you, Mrs. Lamb," Caroline said, dismissing the woman before her mother remembered the salad dressing.

A call to her sister didn't produce any better results.

"I have no time to keep up with your social schedule, Caroline. You disappeared just after I announced my pregnancy. I assumed you had left in a fit of ousy. But I had no idea you'd go so far as to get nant yourself. Couldn't you let me be firs something?"

Having determined that her sister knew noth about those lost two weeks, Caroline quickly smooth her feathers and hung up the phone. Mrs. Lamb co firmed that her father had called and would be wor ing late, which seemed to be a common occurrence.

No wonder no one knew anything. They barely sav each other. All of them together in her hospital room must have been their version of a family reunion. And not a very happy one.

Caroline crawled into bed and rested on the pillov hoping its softness would soothe her head.

Tomorrow.

Tomorrow she would confront her father. Tom row she would ask more questions, find out about th elusive two weeks.

Tomorrow, she would see Max again.

Max glowered at her as he crossed the threshold, and the other two looked uneasy.

"Are you here to see my father?" she asked Adrian and Prescott.

Before either of them could answer, she heard footsteps behind her, and her father's voice answered.

"They're here as our guests for dinner, of course, just as Mr. Daniels is."

She turned to face him. "Max and I are dining on the patio."

Her father hadn't bothered with her since he brought her home from the hospital, but he smiled now as if they were perfectly in tune. "I know that was your plan, Caro, but I told Mrs. Lamb you'd changed your mind. I thought we'd all dine together."

Several responses ran through Caroline's head, the foremost of which was to kick her father in the shins and grab Max's hand and run. Definitely too immature. And if she challenged his decision and insisted on being served on the patio, it would cause Mrs. Lamb a great deal of trouble. And her father would probably just move his guests to the patio, also.

Leaving her no choice but to grin and bear it.

"I see. My apologies, Max. I'm afraid my plans have gone awry." At least she wanted Max to know she hadn't included her other—whatever they were—in the invitation.

"No problem," he murmured, but he was glaring at Adrian and Prescott, not even looking at her.

Determined to draw his attention, she slipped her hand into his. When he looked down at her, she leaned against him ever so slightly. "I'm glad you came."

His indrawn breath as his gaze fell to her neckline gave her some satisfaction. She grinned when his eyes met hers. At least he wasn't ignoring her now.

"Let's all go to the sun room and have a drink while Mrs. Lamb finishes preparing dinner," James suggested, acting the genial host.

In the sun room, Amelia was sitting in a pool of light from a nearby lamp, industriously stitching.

"Good evening, Mother," Caroline said, wondering if she should offer her a kiss on the cheek. She concluded it probably wasn't a habit. This family, her family, seemed as disconnected as any she'd ever seen.

"Good evening, dear. How are you?"

It gave Caroline a warm feeling to know that her mother hadn't forgotten her physical problems, at least. Perhaps she was wrong to think her family was uninvolved.

"Much better. My headache is almost gone."

"You had a headache? That's unusual, Caroline. You should ask Mrs. Lamb for some aspirin."

So much for the warm fuzzies.

"Caroline is still suffering from her concussion, Amelia," James explained.

"Oh, yes. You were in the hospital. Nasty places, hospitals."

James seemed to suddenly realize everyone but Amelia was still standing. "Please, be seated. I'll serve drinks. Adrian, Prescott, your usual?"

Caroline resented her father's effort to make it clear that the other two were frequent guests. She turned to Max even as she tugged at his hand to lead him to the sofa where her mother sat. "What will you have, Max?"

"What are you having?" he asked.

"My usual," she assured him with a grin, "a club soda."

Her mother continued her stitching, but the men in the room stared at her as if she'd just revealed a national secret.

"What's wrong?"

"How did you know what you usually have?" James demanded, taking several steps toward her.

Realization of what she'd said set in, and she shook her head slowly. "I . . . I don't know."

Her father slapped his palm down on the bar. "Damn it, Caroline, why can't you remember the important things?"

"You think I'm doing it on purpose?" she retorted, irritated by his words. She was just as frustrated as her father at her inability to recall her life.

"Really, James, your behavior is inappropriate," Amelia said, still calmly stitching.

"Sorry."

"Is a club soda what I usually have?" Caroline asked in the silence that followed.

"Yes," Prescott said, speaking for the first time. "You always say alcohol gives you a headache."

Even Max nodded in agreement. "And I'll have the same."

"Mr. Daniels, are you sure you want a club soda? The rest of us are having Scotch," James said.

Max withdrew his hand from Caroline's and rose to walk over to the bar. "A club soda is fine." He picked up the two her father poured and brought them back to Caroline.

"Maybe I'll have a club soda, too," Prescott suddenly said, smiling at Caroline.

She couldn't resist sharing a smile with Max. Poor Prescott was so predictable. And Max's smile was heavenly. Just as she was searching for a reason to take his hand again, the doorbell rang.

"Who could that be?" she asked, looking at her father.

He shrugged his shoulders.

"I would imagine it's your sister," Amelia stated as she continued to stitch. "She doesn't feel like cooking and they haven't found a housekeeper yet."

"How can they afford a housekeeper?" James snapped. "Roddy isn't the most successful stockbroker I've ever seen."

"I told them you would pay for her," Amelia said.

Caroline had to hand it to her mother. In her placid way, she had more effectively matched James than anyone Caroline had ever seen. Her father was gaping like a landed trout.

Chelsea and her husband entered the sun room, pausing at the entrance. "Hello, everybody."

When greetings were offered, Roddy moved forward but Chelsea grabbed his arm to hold him back. "Well? Aren't you going to say something?"

"What would you like to drink?" James asked, turning back to the bar.

"Not that, Daddy!" Chelsea said, pouting. "I'm wearing a maternity dress, my first."

"It's lovely," Caroline murmured, hoping her low-key compliment would satisfy her sister.

"Thank you. When you need maternity clothes, Caro, you'll have to ask me where to shop. I found some of the best places." Chelsea's superior air, while annoying, at least signaled she'd found a way to compensate for Caroline's pregnancy.

Apparently satisfied with the response to her new dress, Chelsea allowed Roddy to lead her to a chair. "Get me some white wine, sweetums," she cooed as she sat down.

"No," Amelia said calmly, but her word had the effect of an explosion. Everyone stared at her.

Even Caroline was taken aback. In the little she had discovered about her mother, she assumed Amelia had nothing to say about anyone's life in her house.

"What? I always have white wine, Mother. And I should be pampered. After all, I'm pregnant." Chelsea pouted again.

"I'm sure your doctor told you to have no alcohol. It's not good for the baby."

"But surely one little glass of wine—" Chelsea began, but her mother cut her off.

"No. Have club soda like your sister."

"Oh, of course! Caroline is always right!" Chelsea huffed, sliding down in her chair and crossing her arms over her chest.

"Your mother's right, darling," Roddy began with such tentative tones that Caroline fought the urge to chime in with encouragement. It wasn't hard to decide who wore the pants in that family, even if they were maternity pants.

"I'm sure Mother heard that rule at the home for unwed mothers. And, of course, *they* shouldn't indulge because they have no self-control, but I—"

"Also have no self-control," James finished. "You'll do as your mother says and have club soda."

Caroline leaned toward Max. "I'm sorry," she whispered. "I'd planned on a private dinner. Then you wouldn't have had to endure this argument."

"No problem."

She stared at him in irritation. The least he could do was look disappointed at having to share her with this mob all evening. Instead, he seemed quite interested in Chelsea's performance.

Maybe he was attracted to Chelsea. Her honey blond curls, even if they were out of a bottle, gave her a little-girl look that some men found alluring. Caroline couldn't remember anything about her relationship with Max, but she knew she didn't want him attracted to her sister.

"Dinner is ready," Mrs. Lamb announced from the doorway.

Amelia put away her needlework and stood to lead the way into the dining room. Beside each plate was a charming china name plate. Caroline was unhappy to discover Max was to be seated at the opposite end of the table from her.

"I'm afraid a mistake has been made, Daddy," she announced, calmly exchanging Max's name with Adrian's. Instead of having her father's two favorites surrounding her, she would have Max as a dinner partner.

"I just thought I'd like an opportunity to visit with our guest, Caro," James protested.

"Some other time, Daddy." She took Max's arm and drew him to the chair at her mother's left. He courteously pulled out the chair beside him for her, in the center of the table, opposite her sister.

Max wasn't sure what difference it made where he sat at the big table. From the moment he'd met the other two men on the front porch, he'd realized the evening would be a disaster. He'd been an idiot to expect anything else, he decided.

An uneasy silence fell on the table as the housekeeper served consommé. Max may not have been brought up in a wealthy mansion, but he'd been taught good manners. He turned to his hostess.

"Do you do needlework for relaxation, Mrs. Adkins?" he asked politely.

His hostess looked surprised at his question, but she smiled. "Why, no. Actually, I'm doing it for an auction the home for the unwed mothers is having to raise money. It's so expensive to care for all of them."

"That's very nice of you," he said, and picked up his soupspoon. As if he'd knocked a hole in a dam, words poured forth from Mrs. Adkins as she described all the ways the money would prove useful for her charity.

An occasional nod or encouraging word was all Max needed to contribute for the next few minutes. That gave him plenty of time to think about the brunette beauty beside him. She'd been on his mind for the past two months. Their two weeks together had been wonderful. Since then he'd wondered if he'd ever see her again.

Maybe he would've been better off if he hadn't.

He sneaked a glance at her and decided that wasn't true. If he had a chance to be with Caroline, then he wanted that chance.

"Do you have brothers or sisters, Mr. Daniels?" Mrs. Adkins asked.

"Why, yes, ma'am. I have three brothers and two sisters."

"My, you come from a large family. Do they all work with you at your business? I believe my husband said you build homes?"

Max noticed Caroline leaned a little closer, as if trying to hear what they were saying. He grinned. She'd loved to hear him talk of his family. He'd assumed she had none of her own, but now he wondered if it was because hers seemed so distant to each other.

"Only my baby sister, Susan. She answers the phone when she's not in class."

"She's in high school?"

"No, Susan's a junior in college."

"Was she the one who answered the phone when I called yesterday?" Caroline asked, proving that she'd been listening to their conversation.

"Yeah."

"Did—did I meet her when we—while we were dating?"

"No."

He hadn't wanted to share her with his family. One introduction and they would've taken her in like a long-lost relative. So he'd put off taking her home to his mother. Until it was too late.

"Did I meet any of your family?"

"No."

Her hazel eyes, with their dark lashes, rounded in surprise. He wanted to lean toward her and kiss her soft lips and tease her about her reaction. Instead, he sat stiffly, unsure what to say. How could he explain the sweetness he'd wanted to hold close, keep private, as long as possible?

"And you had the nerve to complain that I didn't tell you about my family?" she whispered to him under her breath so her mother couldn't hear.

"At least I *told* you about my family."

"That's going to be a little hard to prove since I can't even remember *you,* much less what you told me!"

"Caroline," her father called, pulling her attention away from Max.

"Yes?"

"I wondered if you wanted to have lunch with me tomorrow? You haven't been to the office since the accident, and you used to come all the time."

"She can't," Amelia said as she rang the bell for the next course to be served. "Tomorrow is her day at the home for the unwed mothers."

"It is?" Caroline asked, seemingly surprised.

"I really don't think that's appropriate now, Mother," Chelsea said. "After all, they might mistake Caro for one of the inmates and not let her leave at the end of the day." She giggled, as if feeling her words were quite entertaining, but no one else laughed.

Max thought it best to ignore her remark. "What do you do there?" he asked Caroline.

The lost look on her face made him want to take her into his arms and comfort her, but that wouldn't be ap-

propriate dinner behavior. Besides, anything she did got
that reaction from him.

"I—I don't know. Mother, what exactly do I do
there?"

"Why, Caro, you've done some wonderful things.
You teach a cooking class, and you pay for a hairdresser to give free haircuts, and you teach them to
read, too. Mrs. Brown is thrilled with your help."

"A cooking class? I know how to cook?"

"Oh, nothing fancy. That's why it's so good. You
teach them how to make easy, well-balanced meals.
Mrs. Lamb helped you."

In spite of the confusion on Caroline's face, Max
wasn't surprised. She'd done a little cooking at his
house. Nothing fancy, but good wholesome food. Even
more interesting, she'd never acted as if she expected to
be waited on. Maybe that's why he found her real identity so difficult to believe.

He'd dated one or two well-to-do young ladies after
he'd begun to make his mark in the world. Any man
making money drew that type of woman. In fact,
Chelsea reminded him of them. And Chelsea, or anyone like her, would never fit into his family.

Caroline, on the other hand, would be adored by his
sisters, and if it were anyone but him who introduced
her, his brothers would be fighting over her. Just like the
two jerks at the table.

Prescott, sitting on Caroline's left, leaned toward her.
"It shouldn't surprise you that you can cook, Caroline. You do everything well."

"I'm not sure Caroline should do anything so strenuous just yet," James said.

"You'd better eat some lunch, child. You don't look too well. And you've got a baby to think about now."

Caroline smiled faintly. It was too easy to forget that she was carrying a child inside her, since she couldn't remember the event that had brought it about. But Mrs. Lamb was right. She needed to eat.

"Let's take the tray back downstairs. I've had enough eating in bed to last me awhile."

And she needed to calm down again before she faced her father. He had some explaining to do.

SHE DIDN'T GET TO ASK her father any questions that night. Long before he'd returned from the office, she'd gone to bed, exhausted. Her mother had gotten home around four, but her vagueness made Caroline wonder if she even remembered that her daughter had come home from the hospital that day.

Even so, Caroline tried to question her at the dinner table that evening.

"Uh, Mother?"

"Yes, dear?" Amelia replied distractedly, examining the salad she was eating.

"Do you know why I argued with my father?"

"Did you? I have no idea, dear. You argue with him frequently, even though I tell you you shouldn't." She took a bite of salad and chewed it consideringly. "I don't think Mrs. Lamb is using a dietetic dressing, even though I asked her to."

"Please think, Mother. It's important."

"I know it is. I gained two pounds last month, and I'm sure it's the salad dressing."

"No, I mean arguing with—with my father." She had no idea what she normally called him.

Amelia looked at her blankly. "About what? Was he difficult when he picked you up?"

"No, not today," Caroline said, hoping her patience could withstand more conversation with her mother. "Mrs. Lamb said that I had a fight with him a little over two months ago, and then I left."

"Did you? Where did you go?"

Caroline sighed. "I don't know. Didn't you notice I was gone?"

"Hmm. Two months ago? I think that's when I went to that spa in Arizona." She laid down her fork and rang the dinner bell that rested on the table by her plate.

Mrs. Lamb opened the door that led to the kitchen. "Yes, ma'am?"

"Mrs. Lamb, didn't I go to that spa at the end of June?" Amelia asked.

"Was that when I left, while Mother was at the spa?" Caroline added, hoping to clarify matters.

"That's right. Your mother left the day before you did."

"Where did Caroline go, Mrs. Lamb? She wants to know."

The housekeeper looked at Caroline and then her mother. "I don't know, ma'am. She didn't say."

"Thank you, Mrs. Lamb," Caroline said, dismissing the woman before her mother remembered the salad dressing.

A call to her sister didn't produce any better results.

"I have no time to keep up with your social schedule, Caroline. You disappeared just after I announced my pregnancy. I assumed you had left in a fit of jealousy. But I had no idea you'd go so far as to get pregnant yourself. Couldn't you let me be first in *something?*"

Having determined that her sister knew nothing about those lost two weeks, Caroline quickly smoothed her feathers and hung up the phone. Mrs. Lamb confirmed that her father had called and would be working late, which seemed to be a common occurrence.

No wonder no one knew anything. They barely saw each other. All of them together in her hospital room must have been their version of a family reunion. And not a very happy one.

Caroline crawled into bed and rested on the pillow, hoping its softness would soothe her head.

Tomorrow.

Tomorrow she would confront her father. Tomorrow she would ask more questions, find out about those elusive two weeks.

Tomorrow, she would see Max again.

Chapter Four

The first dress had to be replaced when she discovered it was too tight.

Fortunately, she made another discovery—an emerald green silk dress, with a V neckline that dipped dangerously low. The flowing skirt ended right at the knees and fluttered every time she moved. If he was a leg man, she'd definitely get his attention.

Max Daniels may have thought she'd tortured him before, but he hadn't seen anything yet.

After perfecting her makeup, she ran downstairs and poked her head through the kitchen door. "Everything okay?"

Mrs. Lamb, working at the huge sink, smiled distractedly. "Oh, yes."

"Thanks. I'll get the doorbell when it rings."

She didn't have long to wait.

Speeding to the front door, she threw it open, a welcoming smile on her face. It faltered when she discovered not one handsome man, but three, on the doorstep.

And none of them looked happy.

"Uh, come in," she muttered, stepping back.

Max glowered at her as he crossed the threshold, and the other two looked uneasy.

"Are you here to see my father?" she asked Adrian and Prescott.

Before either of them could answer, she heard footsteps behind her, and her father's voice answered.

"They're here as our guests for dinner, of course, just as Mr. Daniels is."

She turned to face him. "Max and I are dining on the patio."

Her father hadn't bothered with her since he brought her home from the hospital, but he smiled now as if they were perfectly in tune. "I know that was your plan, Caro, but I told Mrs. Lamb you'd changed your mind. I thought we'd all dine together."

Several responses ran through Caroline's head, the foremost of which was to kick her father in the shins and grab Max's hand and run. Definitely too immature. And if she challenged his decision and insisted on being served on the patio, it would cause Mrs. Lamb a great deal of trouble. And her father would probably just move his guests to the patio, also.

Leaving her no choice but to grin and bear it.

"I see. My apologies, Max. I'm afraid my plans have gone awry." At least she wanted Max to know she hadn't included her other—whatever they were—in the invitation.

"No problem," he murmured, but he was glaring at Adrian and Prescott, not even looking at her.

Determined to draw his attention, she slipped her hand into his. When he looked down at her, she leaned against him ever so slightly. "I'm glad you came."

His indrawn breath as his gaze fell to her neckline gave her some satisfaction. She grinned when his eyes met hers. At least he wasn't ignoring her now.

"Let's all go to the sun room and have a drink while Mrs. Lamb finishes preparing dinner," James suggested, acting the genial host.

In the sun room, Amelia was sitting in a pool of light from a nearby lamp, industriously stitching.

"Good evening, Mother," Caroline said, wondering if she should offer her a kiss on the cheek. She concluded it probably wasn't a habit. This family, her family, seemed as disconnected as any she'd ever seen.

"Good evening, dear. How are you?"

It gave Caroline a warm feeling to know that her mother hadn't forgotten her physical problems, at least. Perhaps she was wrong to think her family was uninvolved.

"Much better. My headache is almost gone."

"You had a headache? That's unusual, Caroline. You should ask Mrs. Lamb for some aspirin."

So much for the warm fuzzies.

"Caroline is still suffering from her concussion, Amelia," James explained.

"Oh, yes. You were in the hospital. Nasty places, hospitals."

James seemed to suddenly realize everyone but Amelia was still standing. "Please, be seated. I'll serve drinks. Adrian, Prescott, your usual?"

Caroline resented her father's effort to make it clear that the other two were frequent guests. She turned to Max even as she tugged at his hand to lead him to the sofa where her mother sat. "What will you have, Max?"

"What are you having?" he asked.

"My usual," she assured him with a grin, "a club soda."

Her mother continued her stitching, but the men in the room stared at her as if she'd just revealed a national secret.

"What's wrong?"

"How did you know what you usually have?" James demanded, taking several steps toward her.

Realization of what she'd said set in, and she shook her head slowly. "I . . . I don't know."

Her father slapped his palm down on the bar. "Damn it, Caroline, why can't you remember the important things?"

"You think I'm doing it on purpose?" she retorted, irritated by his words. She was just as frustrated as her father at her inability to recall her life.

"Really, James, your behavior is inappropriate," Amelia said, still calmly stitching.

"Sorry."

"Is a club soda what I usually have?" Caroline asked in the silence that followed.

"Yes," Prescott said, speaking for the first time. "You always say alcohol gives you a headache."

Even Max nodded in agreement. "And I'll have the same."

"Mr. Daniels, are you sure you want a club soda? The rest of us are having Scotch," James said.

Max withdrew his hand from Caroline's and rose to walk over to the bar. "A club soda is fine." He picked up the two her father poured and brought them back to Caroline.

"Maybe I'll have a club soda, too," Prescott suddenly said, smiling at Caroline.

She couldn't resist sharing a smile with Max. Poor Prescott was so predictable. And Max's smile was heavenly. Just as she was searching for a reason to take his hand again, the doorbell rang.

"Who could that be?" she asked, looking at her father.

He shrugged his shoulders.

"I would imagine it's your sister," Amelia stated as she continued to stitch. "She doesn't feel like cooking and they haven't found a housekeeper yet."

"How can they afford a housekeeper?" James snapped. "Roddy isn't the most successful stockbroker I've ever seen."

"I told them you would pay for her," Amelia said.

Caroline had to hand it to her mother. In her placid way, she had more effectively matched James than anyone Caroline had ever seen. Her father was gaping like a landed trout.

Chelsea and her husband entered the sun room, pausing at the entrance. "Hello, everybody."

When greetings were offered, Roddy moved forward but Chelsea grabbed his arm to hold him back. "Well? Aren't you going to say something?"

"What would you like to drink?" James asked, turning back to the bar.

"Not that, Daddy!" Chelsea said, pouting. "I'm wearing a maternity dress, my first."

"It's lovely," Caroline murmured, hoping her low-key compliment would satisfy her sister.

"Thank you. When you need maternity clothes, Caro, you'll have to ask me where to shop. I found some of the best places." Chelsea's superior air, while annoying, at least signaled she'd found a way to compensate for Caroline's pregnancy.

Apparently satisfied with the response to her new dress, Chelsea allowed Roddy to lead her to a chair. "Get me some white wine, sweetums," she cooed as she sat down.

"No," Amelia said calmly, but her word had the effect of an explosion. Everyone stared at her.

Even Caroline was taken aback. In the little she had discovered about her mother, she assumed Amelia had nothing to say about anyone's life in her house.

"What? I always have white wine, Mother. And I should be pampered. After all, I'm pregnant." Chelsea pouted again.

"I'm sure your doctor told you to have no alcohol. It's not good for the baby."

"But surely one little glass of wine—" Chelsea began, but her mother cut her off.

"No. Have club soda like your sister."

"Oh, of course! Caroline is always right!" Chelsea huffed, sliding down in her chair and crossing her arms over her chest.

"Your mother's right, darling," Roddy began with such tentative tones that Caroline fought the urge to chime in with encouragement. It wasn't hard to decide who wore the pants in that family, even if they were maternity pants.

"I'm sure Mother heard that rule at the home for unwed mothers. And, of course, *they* shouldn't indulge because they have no self-control, but I—"

"Also have no self-control," James finished. "You'll do as your mother says and have club soda."

Caroline leaned toward Max. "I'm sorry," she whispered. "I'd planned on a private dinner. Then you wouldn't have had to endure this argument."

"No problem."

She stared at him in irritation. The least he could do was look disappointed at having to share her with this mob all evening. Instead, he seemed quite interested in Chelsea's performance.

Maybe he was attracted to Chelsea. Her honey blond curls, even if they were out of a bottle, gave her a little-girl look that some men found alluring. Caroline couldn't remember anything about her relationship with Max, but she knew she didn't want him attracted to her sister.

"Dinner is ready," Mrs. Lamb announced from the doorway.

Amelia put away her needlework and stood to lead the way into the dining room. Beside each plate was a charming china name plate. Caroline was unhappy to discover Max was to be seated at the opposite end of the table from her.

"I'm afraid a mistake has been made, Daddy," she announced, calmly exchanging Max's name with Adrian's. Instead of having her father's two favorites surrounding her, she would have Max as a dinner partner.

"I just thought I'd like an opportunity to visit with our guest, Caro," James protested.

"Some other time, Daddy." She took Max's arm and drew him to the chair at her mother's left. He courteously pulled out the chair beside him for her, in the center of the table, opposite her sister.

Max wasn't sure what difference it made where he sat at the big table. From the moment he'd met the other two men on the front porch, he'd realized the evening would be a disaster. He'd been an idiot to expect anything else, he decided.

An uneasy silence fell on the table as the housekeeper served consommé. Max may not have been brought up in a wealthy mansion, but he'd been taught good manners. He turned to his hostess.

"Do you do needlework for relaxation, Mrs. Adkins?" he asked politely.

His hostess looked surprised at his question, but she smiled. "Why, no. Actually, I'm doing it for an auction the home for the unwed mothers is having to raise money. It's so expensive to care for all of them."

"That's very nice of you," he said, and picked up his soupspoon. As if he'd knocked a hole in a dam, words poured forth from Mrs. Adkins as she described all the ways the money would prove useful for her charity.

An occasional nod or encouraging word was all Max needed to contribute for the next few minutes. That gave him plenty of time to think about the brunette beauty beside him. She'd been on his mind for the past two months. Their two weeks together had been wonderful. Since then he'd wondered if he'd ever see her again.

Maybe he would've been better off if he hadn't.

He sneaked a glance at her and decided that wasn't true. If he had a chance to be with Caroline, then he wanted that chance.

"Do you have brothers or sisters, Mr. Daniels?" Mrs. Adkins asked.

"Why, yes, ma'am. I have three brothers and two sisters."

"My, you come from a large family. Do they all work with you at your business? I believe my husband said you build homes?"

Max noticed Caroline leaned a little closer, as if trying to hear what they were saying. He grinned. She'd loved to hear him talk of his family. He'd assumed she had none of her own, but now he wondered if it was because hers seemed so distant to each other.

"Only my baby sister, Susan. She answers the phone when she's not in class."

"She's in high school?"

"No, Susan's a junior in college."

"Was she the one who answered the phone when I called yesterday?" Caroline asked, proving that she'd been listening to their conversation.

"Yeah."

"Did—did I meet her when we—while we were dating?"

"No."

He hadn't wanted to share her with his family. One introduction and they would've taken her in like a long-lost relative. So he'd put off taking her home to his mother. Until it was too late.

"Did I meet any of your family?"

"No."

Her hazel eyes, with their dark lashes, rounded in surprise. He wanted to lean toward her and kiss her soft lips and tease her about her reaction. Instead, he sat stiffly, unsure what to say. How could he explain the sweetness he'd wanted to hold close, keep private, as long as possible?

"And you had the nerve to complain that I didn't tell you about my family?" she whispered to him under her breath so her mother couldn't hear.

"At least I *told* you about my family."

"That's going to be a little hard to prove since I can't even remember *you,* much less what you told me!"

"Caroline," her father called, pulling her attention away from Max.

"Yes?"

"I wondered if you wanted to have lunch with me tomorrow? You haven't been to the office since the accident, and you used to come all the time."

"She can't," Amelia said as she rang the bell for the next course to be served. "Tomorrow is her day at the home for the unwed mothers."

"It is?" Caroline asked, seemingly surprised.

"I really don't think that's appropriate now, Mother," Chelsea said. "After all, they might mistake Caro for one of the inmates and not let her leave at the end of the day." She giggled, as if feeling her words were quite entertaining, but no one else laughed.

Max thought it best to ignore her remark. "What do you do there?" he asked Caroline.

The lost look on her face made him want to take her into his arms and comfort her, but that wouldn't be ap-

propriate dinner behavior. Besides, anything she did got that reaction from him.

"I—I don't know. Mother, what exactly do I do there?"

"Why, Caro, you've done some wonderful things. You teach a cooking class, and you pay for a hairdresser to give free haircuts, and you teach them to read, too. Mrs. Brown is thrilled with your help."

"A cooking class? I know how to cook?"

"Oh, nothing fancy. That's why it's so good. You teach them how to make easy, well-balanced meals. Mrs. Lamb helped you."

In spite of the confusion on Caroline's face, Max wasn't surprised. She'd done a little cooking at his house. Nothing fancy, but good wholesome food. Even more interesting, she'd never acted as if she expected to be waited on. Maybe that's why he found her real identity so difficult to believe.

He'd dated one or two well-to-do young ladies after he'd begun to make his mark in the world. Any man making money drew that type of woman. In fact, Chelsea reminded him of them. And Chelsea, or anyone like her, would never fit into his family.

Caroline, on the other hand, would be adored by his sisters, and if it were anyone but him who introduced her, his brothers would be fighting over her. Just like the two jerks at the table.

Prescott, sitting on Caroline's left, leaned toward her. "It shouldn't surprise you that you can cook, Caroline. You do everything well."

"I'm not sure Caroline should do anything so strenuous just yet," James said.

Max smiled in amusement as he watched Caroline's chin rise. Only once had he tried to tell her what to do. Her reaction had taught him a lot about her.

"I'm sure I'll be just fine. What time do I usually go, Mother, and—and where is it?"

"I'll send Lewis back home to drive you if you insist on going," James said, irritation in his voice.

Doubt darkened Caroline's hazel eyes. Max guessed she had just realized that the city she'd grown up in was strange to her, and she could easily get lost. In an attempt to comfort her, he took her right hand in his and squeezed it gently.

Her gaze as she turned to him reminded him all over again why he was here, dining with the ill-assorted group. The warmth in Caroline's eyes lit a fire in him that would never die.

Mrs. Lamb brought in the main course and everyone turned their attention to eating. About halfway through the meal, Caroline abruptly excused herself and fled the table, her hand to her mouth.

Max stood to go after her, but James Adkins ordered him back to the table. "Chelsea," he barked, "see about your sister."

"Me?" she asked in horror. "I can't, Daddy. If I do, I'll lose my dinner, too. She's just experiencing temporary morning sickness."

Max was willing to bet everything he owned that Chelsea hadn't been so calmly accepting of the nausea when it was happening to her. "I'll go," he said, as he stood again. "I've helped my sister a couple of times."

"But it's not morning," Prescott said, confusion in his voice as Max left the room. "Is that normal?"

While Max followed the sounds of someone throwing up, he marveled at his desire to help Caroline through her nausea. He was notorious in his family for his weak stomach. But he wanted to be at Caroline's side now, to share her difficulties. To experience the growth of his child in her.

The only problem was, he wasn't sure it was his child.

He shoved that disturbing thought aside and rapped on the bathroom door. "Caroline?"

She moaned before muttering faintly, "Go away."

Pushing the door open, he took in the pitiful sight of Caroline bent over the toilet. Without bothering to ask her opinion, he slid into the small room and wrapped one supporting arm around her waist and laid a hand on her forehead.

As another wave of nausea hit her, she sagged against him, moaning. When it ended, he held her to him and reached for a washcloth. After wetting it, he wiped her face gently. Then he offered her a glass of water to rinse her mouth.

"How did you know what I needed?" she asked afterward. "It was almost as if you've been through morning sickness before."

He ran a finger down the side of her beautiful cheek, enjoying the opportunity to hold her again, even in these circumstances. "That's because I have."

It didn't occur to him what she would think until she stiffened and her face clouded over.

Chapter Five

Caroline's heart sank. She'd wanted Max to be the father of her baby because of the strong attraction she felt for him. But his answer brought home to her how little she knew about Max Daniels.

Or herself.

"With my sister, Caroline, with my sister," he hurriedly said. "Her husband traveled a lot during the early months of her pregnancy and she stayed with us."

"Oh," was all she could think to say since she was overcome with relief. She still didn't know enough about Max, she warned herself, but the happiness filling her mocked that thought.

"Oh," she repeated. "I thought you meant—"

"No," he said hurriedly as he ran his hands up and down her arms. "I've never—I mean, you're the only—"

"I'm glad." Understatement of the year. She'd die of jealousy if he even so much as thought of another woman.

"There's not too many people I'd risk nausea for," he added. "You should count yourself lucky."

"Me and your sister? Is that all?"

"Maybe my mother or Susan. Or one of my brothers, though they won't be experiencing morning sickness," he said with a laugh.

"You're very close to your family?"

"Yeah."

"Then why didn't you introduce me to any of them?" she asked. She couldn't ask that question in front of her mother, but she was dying to know the answer.

He sighed and linked his hands behind her back, bringing her body closer to him. "Because I didn't want to share you. What we had—have—is very special. My family kind of takes over, and I wanted you all to myself."

"Oh."

He frowned. "Don't you believe me?"

She wanted to. With all her heart she wanted to. But there was so much she didn't know, didn't understand, didn't remember. "I—I don't know."

"Then I guess I'll just have to show you," he murmured.

His blue eyes invited her to come closer and she met him more than halfway, leaning against his broad chest, loving his solid warmth, his all-male scent. His caring about her enough to face her sickness warmed her, but not nearly as much as the way his lips were coming closer and closer. She closed her eyes, anticipating his touch, her heart racing.

"Caroline?" Mrs. Lamb called out as she pushed the bathroom door ajar.

Caroline's eyes popped open and she saw the embarrassment she was feeling in Max's blue ones. He took his hands away and stepped back from her.

"Your mother sent me to see if you were all right," Mrs. Lamb explained, but her gaze was on Max.

"I'll—I'll go back to the dining room and leave you to Mrs. Lamb's capable hands," Max said, and ducked out of the room.

"Thank you!" Caroline called out, wishing he was still there, holding her.

"What a nice man," Mrs. Lamb said, and then clucked in sympathy. "You do look a sight, and it's all my fault."

Caroline whirled to stare at herself in the mirror, concerned with how Max saw her, before Mrs. Lamb's words registered. "Your fault? Why is it your fault? I would've thought it was the baby's fault, or the fault of one of those three men sitting so calmly eating their dinner right now."

Caroline's nausea wasn't helping her temper. Nor the thought that Max had seen her when she wasn't at her best. Even more irritating was the frustration she was feeling because Max hadn't been able to demonstrate the magic they shared. "It's not fair that only the woman tosses her cookies in this pregnancy business. Why can't the man get sick, too?"

"Well, now, some men do experience a similar nausea, but not many. Anyway, I shouldn't have put jalapeño peppers in the beans, but that's your father's favorite and I just forgot about you being pregnant."

Caroline attempted to restore some order to her hair as she asked, "You think that's what caused it?"

"Oh, yes. I did the same thing to Chelsea before she even knew she was pregnant. Now, you just come back to the table and eat a little more. You've got to keep up your strength. But avoid the beans."

Mrs. Lamb left the bathroom and Caroline sat on the side of the bathtub to consider her options. She'd rather pass up a return to the dinner table. Except for Max.

Even though she knew she'd have little opportunity to question him, she couldn't resist being near him. Not that he'd feel any attraction for her now. How sexy can it be to lose your dinner at any moment?

But, she realized with a sigh, she was really hungry now. She had to eat something. Slipping up to her room, she renewed her makeup and hurried back to the dining room.

Max stood as she entered and everyone else stared at her. When she sat down again, he leaned over and whispered, "Better now?"

Though she appreciated his concern, her embarrassment kept her from showing him. She gave an abrupt nod and sipped the ice tea by her plate.

"Sorry, Caro, I should've warned you about the beans," Chelsea said, sincere regret in her voice.

Caroline looked up in surprise. She hadn't expected such sympathy from her younger sister. "Mrs. Lamb mentioned that you'd had an encounter with them, too."

"Yes. Miserable, isn't it? But after the first three months, it goes away."

"Not always," Amelia said. "Your father got quite tired of my dashing away from the table."

"I think he should've been grateful he wasn't the one having to do the dashing," Caroline muttered.

"Women are the stronger sex," Adrian said, speaking for almost the first time that evening. "I think that's why they bear the responsibility for continuing the human race." He smiled at Caroline, almost convincing her of his sincerity. Then he added, "Our child is going to have a wonderful mother."

Prescott immediately protested, but Max said nothing. Caroline stole a glance at him to see the steely glare he was directing Adrian's way. If she'd been Adrian, she would make sure she steered wide of Max.

"Are you the father of Caroline's baby?" Amelia asked, as if she were discussing the weather.

"Of course I am. I said I was from the beginning," Adrian replied, equally calm.

"You can't prove that," Prescott retorted, leaning across the table.

"Not until after the baby is born and we can do DNA testing," Adrian agreed. "But I intend to prove to Caroline that I'm the father long before that. I don't want my child to be born illegitimately."

Caroline stared at Adrian, her heart sinking. Could the man lie so sincerely? And could he be the father of her child? She didn't want him to be. Already she knew she wanted Max to be the father of the baby she was carrying. But what if he wasn't?

Sudden movement beside her drew her attention. Max, his expression grim, was about to say something. She slid her hand beneath the tablecloth to rest on his thigh, sending a pleading look his way.

He leaned back in his chair, his gaze resting on her, questioning her, and she silently shook her head. She didn't want a fight here and now, when she knew so little about her past.

Most frightening of all were the chills that raced up her arm from touching him. And the desire to continue to do so. How could she want one man so much when another was claiming to be her lover?

"I hope you prove you're the daddy immediately," James said to Adrian, satisfaction in his voice. "I expect to hold a wedding right away, before she has to start wearing maternity clothes like her sister. You hear me, Caroline?"

"I'm sure everyone heard you, Daddy," Caroline said, and forced herself to take another bite of her dinner. Though Prescott continued to sputter, no one else challenged Adrian's assertion.

Max asked Roddy about his position as a stock broker and her brother-in-law talked for several minutes about the stock market. Caroline started to remove her hand from Max's warm thigh, but his left hand settled over hers, trapping it there.

Maybe he'd noticed her dress after all.

THE EVENING GREW increasingly strained. When dinner was finished, they returned to the sun room for coffee. But shortly after taking a cup, Max set it down on the coffee table and stood to leave.

"Thank you for your hospitality, Mr. and Mrs. Adkins, but I have an early appointment in the morning."

"We're glad you could join us," Amelia said politely, her interest again taken with her stitching.

"I'll walk you to the door," Caroline said, standing also. She hoped she might at least have a few minutes alone with him. To talk, of course.

"I'll go with you," James said, walking toward them.

"That's not necessary, Daddy," Caroline retorted.

"Oh, yes, it is. I wouldn't want to be thought rude to one of my guests."

The three of them left the others in the sun room and walked to the front door, Caroline fuming with every step. Once there, Max offered his hand to James and again said thanks.

James didn't take the hint. He stood there, a genial smile on his lips, watching them.

"Thank you for coming, Max, and for—for helping me," Caroline said, giving up on her father's departure. "It didn't turn out exactly as I planned."

"I know. But I enjoyed seeing you again."

Drat the man, he was turning to leave. Caroline grabbed the lapels of his blue suit and pulled him toward her. Ignoring her father's stare, she moved her lips over Max's until he abruptly took control of the kiss, wrapping his arms around her and lifting her up against him.

She released his lapels and encircled his neck, her heart thumping in her chest as she relished the feel of him against her. When he let her slide down his body until her feet touched the floor again, she almost cried out at their separation.

Before taking his arms from around her, he whispered a husky "Goodnight, Caroline," kissed her briefly again, and then walked out the door.

"Well, I didn't know you were so bold, Caro," her father commented, still standing beside her.

Reluctantly Caroline closed the door and turned to face him. "I suggested you remain in the sun room, Daddy."

"I'm glad I didn't. Who knows what advantage that man would've taken of you if I hadn't been here."

Or what advantage I would've taken of *him*, Caroline thought.

"Don't expect me to thank you for the protection, Daddy. It was unwanted."

"You'd better think seriously, young lady, about taking up with one man while carrying another one's child. Adrian might not be as understanding as me."

"We don't know that it's Adrian's baby," she snapped, her heart faltering at the possibility.

"He sounded pretty sure of himself tonight."

"They've all sounded sure of themselves."

"Max didn't protest. Only Prescott."

But he'd wanted to. She shivered as she remembered touching him.

When she remained silent, James said, "I want this matter resolved right away. I was serious about getting you married before you start showing."

"I'll marry when I've discovered who the father is, and not before."

"I have your word on it?" James asked.

"Of course!" Only after her word was given did she have second thoughts. What if the father really was Adrian . . . or Prescott?

"Good," James replied with a smile, as if he'd won, and turned to go back to the sun room.

"Wait! Daddy, what did we argue about two months ago?"

He paused, as if frozen in motion, and then turned slowly. "I don't know what you're talking about."

"Oh, yes, you do. And I want an answer. Mrs. Lamb said we had an argument two months ago, or perhaps two and a half months. The next day I left and didn't return for two weeks. What did we argue about?"

"We're always arguing, Caro. And you frequently go on trips. It seems to me the argument was something about taking up a career. Or getting married. I don't really remember." With another smile, he strolled down the hall.

Caroline stared after him, her gut feeling telling her he was lying. And yet, either of those subjects might have come up. She had a feeling her father had been pressuring her about both of them. After all, she was twenty-seven. Her sister, three years younger, was already married.

Wearily she leaned back against the door. It had been a long evening, and she didn't feel up to returning to the sun room. She pushed away from the door and trudged to the stairs, taking them slowly.

Having a baby seemed to sap all her energy.

Or maybe it wasn't the baby's fault. Maybe it was the daddies. All of them.

Now that she'd given her word to her father to marry as soon as proof could be found, she had to make sure the proof featured a tall, dark-haired, blue-eyed man whose slightest touch sent her up in flames.

MAX OVERSLEPT the next morning, after spending most of the night alternating between reliving his night of passion with Caroline two long months ago and trying to figure out how to prove his identity as father of the baby.

The ringing phone brought him awake.

"Hello?" he growled.

"Max, where are you?" Susan demanded, her voice bright and wide-awake.

He checked his watch and groaned. "I was asleep."

"But you have an appointment with Mr. Lawson at the bank in ten minutes."

"Yeah. Call him and tell him something came up. Try to reschedule it for tomorrow."

"Okay."

Before she could hang up, Max said, "Wait, Susan."

"Yes?"

He pondered his question.

"Max? What is it?"

"Did I ever talk to you about Caroline?"

"Caroline Adkins?"

His heart leaped. Had he talked about her and then forgotten he'd done so? Would it convince Caroline that they'd spent two weeks together? "Yes," he replied anxiously.

"Nope."

"Then how did you know who I was talking about?"

"Jim mentioned something about her a couple of months ago, and then she called yesterday." She paused and then, with sisterly cunning, asked, "Is she important?"

"Yeah. And if she calls, find me, wherever I am, okay?"

"Sure. Will I like her?"

"Suze, call the banker, and mind your own business." He almost hung up before he remembered one more warning. "And don't even think about mentioning her name to Mom or Karen, or your job is history."

As he showered and shaved, he thought back over the two weeks he'd shared with Caroline. He'd given her the names of his design firms. If she applied at one of those firms, using his name as a reference, that would be something, at least. Some proof that she knew him.

A few minutes later, he hung up the phone with a sigh. She hadn't called either firm.

After their first lunch together, he'd taken her out to dinner that same evening. He could get the waiter at Mario's to say she'd been there with Max, but that kind of proof was useless. They'd gone to the movies, to the theater one night. He'd taken time off for picnics in the foothills of the Rockies.

Thinking she was a newcomer to the area, he'd even taken her to tour the mint. He had the ticket stubs from that excursion. But they could've been used by anyone.

Ticket stubs didn't tell about the kisses he'd stolen at the back of the tour group. Or the leisurely dinner afterward when they'd laughed about people's reactions to cold, hard cash. Or the exquisite caresses they'd shared before he left her at her hotel room door.

The hotel!

Of course. At least he could prove she'd stayed in the suburbs near his office. He showered and dressed, then grabbed his billfold and keys and hurried out the door.

A few minutes later, he arrived at the desk in the lobby of the medium-priced hotel he'd come to know well. "Excuse me," he said to the young man with his back to the counter.

"Oh, yes, sir. What kind of room do you need? A single?" The bright smile was perfect for PR, but Max wasn't interested.

"Look, about two months ago, the last week or two of June, a young lady stayed here. I need to see her registration card."

"I'm afraid that's not possible, sir. That's privileged information." The smile was gone and a frown took its place.

He hadn't expected high security. "Okay, I don't have to see the card. Just look and see if you had a Caroline Adkins registered during that time. She stayed in Room 210."

"I don't know," the man said, edging away as if he thought Max were a serial killer.

An older man came out of a door just behind the counter. "Yes, Mike, what's the problem?"

Realizing the clerk had called for reinforcements by some silent signal, Max put on his friendliest smile. "I just need confirmation that Caroline Adkins stayed in Room 210 the last week or two of June."

"I'm sorry, but we don't give out information about our clients."

"Look, I'm asking for *confirmation* of what I already know. I walked Miss Adkins to her room most evenings and waited until she took out her key and entered the room before leaving."

"If that's true, sir, why do you need us to confirm that information?"

Good question. Max was beginning to sweat. "Because Miss Adkins has amnesia from a car accident."

"You mean Caroline Adkins, daughter of James Adkins?" There was a flicker of interest in the man's eyes that Max regretted. "She stayed here, with us?"

"Yes. She did. Could you just check your records?"

"And all you want is for me to tell you you're right? I don't have to put anything in writing?"

The man still seemed reluctant, and Max eased his billfold out of his back pocket. The supervisor's gaze immediately flew to Max's hands and then to the clerk, ostensibly filing papers nearby. "Mike, go to the coffee shop and get me some coffee. I'll cover the desk while you're gone."

As soon as the clerk had walked away, Max slid a twenty-dollar bill across the counter. Without a word the supervisor pocketed the bill and turned to the computer.

"The end of June, you said. Room 210?"

"That's right."

The excitement faded as the man worked the computer keys. Finally he turned to Max with a frown. "I don't know what you're trying to pull, but we show no Caroline Adkins in that room."

"What?" Max wanted to grab the man by the throat. "Then who do you show registered?"

"I'm sorry. I can't—"

Max threw another twenty-dollar bill on the counter. "Yes, you can."

"We had a single woman stay in that room for two weeks. She paid in cash and registered under the name of Leslie McVey."

Max stared at him, stunned. "Leslie McVey? The end of June?"

"Yes. Otherwise, we've only had one- or two-nighters in there. We have a heavy turnover. It's not often a guest stays two weeks."

"Do you remember what Miss McVey looked like?"

"No, I don't. However—" he smiled at Max "—I might be persuaded to do so."

Great. All he needed was for the man to say Max had tried to bribe him to identify Caroline. "No thanks."

He strode from the hotel lobby, disappointed and frustrated. Why had Caroline registered under an assumed name? She hadn't hesitated to use her real name with him.

He looked at his watch and groaned. It was already lunchtime, and he'd accomplished very little. Climbing into his truck, he drove back to his office, only a few minutes away.

"It's about time you showed up," Susan greeted him cheerily. "I was just getting ready to beep you."

"Why? A problem on the job sites?"

"No. Caroline Adkins just called."

"Did you get a number?" he demanded.

Susan's eyes widened. "Hey, don't jump down my throat," she protested. "I asked and she said she'd have to call you later. Something about her not being able to tie up the phone."

"She didn't say where she was?" Even as he asked the question, he remembered her intention to do charity work today. "Bring me a phone book."

"But she didn't say where she was."

"I just remembered. The phone book!" he snapped and continued on to his office. He took a deep breath as he sat down behind the desk, hoping to curb his impatience. It wouldn't take much to make Susan suspicious. And when his little sister suspected a secret, she was hell on wheels until she uncovered it.

"Want me to help you look something up?" Susan offered as she entered his office, watching him as she held out the directory.

"No, I'll manage."

Several minutes later he shouted for his sister. He couldn't find any listing for the Home for Unwed Mothers. He was sure that was what Mrs. Adkins had called it last night.

"Yes, brother?"

"I can't find the telephone number."

She ignored his growl and took the directory with a laugh. "I knew you needed my help. What am I looking for?"

"I think it's called the Home for Unwed Mothers."

His thoughts were all centered on Caroline, but he looked up when his sister gasped.

"Your girlfriend is in a home for unwed mothers? Wait until Mom hears about this!"

Chapter Six

"Don't be ridiculous!" Max snapped.

"I'm not the one being ridiculous. Mom's gonna have a fit if one of her grandchildren is illegitimate. Don't you like this lady?"

"Susan, this is none of your business," Max advised her in stern tones. "Caroline is doing charity work at the home. She is not, I repeat, not living there."

"Oh, so I'm not going to be an aunt?" Susan teased, a big grin on her face.

Her words stopped Max cold. What could he say? Yes, she's pregnant. But no, it may not be his baby. That would make a good impression, sure to be passed on to his mother.

"Look, Susan, I want you to forget this conversation ever took place, okay?"

"Sure, no problem. But it'll cost you."

Long years of dealing with his baby sister told him to bargain. Threats would get him nowhere. "How much?"

"There's this gorgeous dress I found. I really need it for my date with Stephen."

"How much?" he repeated.

"A hundred and twenty dollars."

"For a dress? You must be kidding?"

"No, and it's worth it. One look at that dress and he'll be on his knees. Haven't you ever seen a dress like that?"

Yeah. Last night. He shook himself free from the picture of Caroline in the green silk. "Okay," he agreed roughly, pulling his billfold from his back pocket. After bribing the hotel man, now he had to bribe his sister. It was turning out to be an expensive day.

"I'll write you a check for a hundred and fifty if you'll go buy me some lunch before you do your shopping."

"Are you staying here the rest of the afternoon?" Her eyes were round with curiosity and Max had the uneasy feeling he should have protested more at her blackmailing him. It made him uncomfortable for anyone to know what a hold Caroline had on him.

"Just until I get a few things accomplished." *And until Caroline calls.*

He pretended to do paperwork until Susan returned with his lunch. Then he munched the barbecue sandwich and let his mind return to its one constant thought, Caroline.

When the phone rang half an hour later, he'd finished his sandwich but gotten almost no work done.

"Hello?"

"Max, it's Caroline."

Like he wouldn't recognize her voice.

"Yeah. Sorry I missed your call earlier."

"I couldn't leave a number because I'm calling from the home where I'm volunteering today. Anyway, I wanted to apologize again for last evening. Daddy can be difficult, you know."

"Yeah, I can tell."

"I wondered if you'd meet me for dinner this evening, so it would just be the two of us. And we could talk. My treat."

Max almost yanked the telephone cord out of the wall. "Are you trying to insult me? Do you think I can't afford a dinner?"

"No, I didn't think that. It's just that *I* invited *you*"

"Regardless. I ate at your house last night. Tonight I'll pay. I'll pick you up at seven."

"Uh, Max, I don't think that's a good idea. I think Daddy might even go so far as to have us followed. Or if not him, Prescott might think of doing that."

"Not Adrian? He's the one who's sure he's the father of your baby." That had been irritating him ever since last night. Had she slept with the man? And Prescott, too? He didn't usually feel he had the right to question his date's past experience, but this was ridiculous.

There was a pause before Caroline answered, and Max realized he'd hurt her feelings. "I'm sorry—" he began.

"Never mind. Maybe this wasn't such a good idea, after all."

"Caroline, I'm sorry. He upset me last night. We need to talk. I'd like to understand what's going on here."

"You know I can't explain it, Max. I've got amnesia!"

"Calm down. I know. Will you meet me at Mario's?"

Again she paused, and he held his breath for her answer.

"Okay. Where is it?"

"You don't know where it is? We always— Sorry, I forgot." He gave her directions, and they agreed to meet at seven. "And Caroline, I'm glad you called."

"Me, too," she whispered before hanging up.

Max sat with the receiver pressed to his ear until the dial tone became too annoying. Man, he had it bad if she could tie him into knots with a brief phone call.

Yeah, he had it bad.

"LEWIS, I REALLY appreciate your picking me up. I called for a taxi, but there was an hour's wait," Caroline explained as she slid into the front seat by her father's driver.

"You're supposed to ride in back, Miss Caroline," Lewis chided.

"I know, but I'd rather ride with you, like I usually do." She smiled at him until she saw the curious look that she was coming to hate. "No, I don't know why I remembered that. Things, unimportant things, just come to me." She sighed. "Ooh! This is so frustrating."

"Yeah, I guess so. Do you want to go home?"

"Yes, please. I need to change clothes before I go out."

"Will you need me to drive you?"

"No, I'm going to drive myself." She thought about asking him not to mention her outing to her father, but she didn't want to put him into such a difficult position. James Adkins could be harsh if an employee didn't do exactly as he wished. Better not to call attention to her plans and hope Lewis wouldn't think anything about it.

The rush hour in Denver had gotten increasingly heavy the past few years. Cars were backed up quite a way behind them. Caroline was looking over her shoulder at the line of traffic when the limo suddenly jerked and skidded before Lewis quickly corrected it.

"What's wrong?"

The chauffeur eased the limo onto the shoulder of the road and came to a stop. "I think we've got a flat tire."

"Will it take long to fix it?" she asked, automatically looking at her watch. She'd left the home later than she'd intended and it was almost six now.

"No. I'll hurry."

She felt guilty sitting in comfort in the limo as Lewis did the dirty work. Opening her door, she swung her feet to the pavement and stood up.

"Uh, Miss Caroline, we have a problem."

"What is it, Lewis?"

"Two tires are flat. I must've hit something in the road, but I didn't see it."

Seeing the worry on his face, she quickly reassured him. "Don't worry about it, Lewis. I'm not running that late."

"I don't think you understand. I don't have two spares. Only one. I'll have to call for a tow truck, and there are only a few that can handle a limo."

Now she understood. And if she didn't know better, she'd think her father had planned this incident, too. He was determined to keep her away from Max.

"Okay," she said with a sigh. "So you call a tow truck, and then I'll call a taxi. It will be all right, Lewis."

Both of them made their calls, and they each discovered they would have to wait.

"I sure am sorry, Miss Caroline," Lewis said softly when they'd both returned to the limo.

"I know, Lewis." Her mind was dwelling on the man waiting for her at the restaurant, but it suddenly occurred to her that the flat tires provided her with an excellent opportunity to quiz Lewis.

"Lewis, do you remember when I left home two months ago? I was gone for about two weeks."

"Yes, Miss Caroline."

"Do you know why I left, or where I went?"

"No, I don't. I didn't drive you the day you left."

"Did my father say anything? Complain about me?"

Lewis grinned. "He's always complaining about you, Miss Caroline. You know how he is."

"I know," she agreed with a sigh. How she knew.

Suddenly she remembered a scene, a year or two ago, she thought, between her and her father. She'd been his son, the son he'd always wanted, following him into his business, acting as his right-hand man. Until she'd realized she wasn't enjoying her work. In fact she hated it.

When she'd told her father, he'd been heartbroken. That's why she was still living at home. He'd allowed her to return to school and pick up a degree in interior design if she promised not to move out.

"It would upset your mother," he had said gruffly, but she'd known he meant himself.

The memory faded and any more questioning was pointless, so she accepted Lewis's offer of a game of gin while they waited. The taxi and the tow truck arrived almost simultaneously. Caroline hoped she'd be able to depart without Lewis hearing her destination, but he walked her to the taxi.

"Where shall I tell the driver to go?" he asked.

"A restaurant in Golden called Mario's."

Without comment, Lewis gave the destination to the driver, apologized again for stranding her and stepped back. She waved goodbye as the taxi pulled out into traffic.

While the driver negotiated their way, Caroline pulled out her makeup bag. So much for the idea of having a quick shower, changing clothes. She'd have to make do with the contents of her makeup bag.

It was a little after seven when she arrived at the restaurant. Though it wasn't a four-star establishment, she liked the look of the place. It had a warmth and intimacy of which she approved, and she didn't feel terribly out of place in her denim jumper.

"Yes, ma'am?" the maître d' said in way of a greeting.

"I'm here to meet Max Daniels. He—"

"Of course. Right this way." The man showed no hesitation, so she figured either Max dined here often or he'd bribed the man outrageously.

The man led her to the back corner of the restaurant where the light was the dimmest. Max rose from the booth and moved aside for her to slide in. When he joined her on the same side, she looked up, surprised.

"If we're going to talk, I don't want to be overheard."

She didn't, either. And she certainly didn't mind close quarters with Max. As long as she could control the wild response he evoked.

"I'm sorry I'm late. Lewis was taking me home in the limo when we had two flat tires."

He gave her a wry look. "Was your father planting nails in the road?"

She tried to look stern, but an answering smile refused to be denied. "No. Though he might have if he'd thought of it."

"I'm not exactly his favorite person."

"No, you're not, but I'm not sure why. I think the two of you have a lot in common." She knew he didn't appreciate her comment by the ferocious frown on his face.

"What do you mean?"

"You both started out small and became a success. You're both very protective . . . and you like to get your way."

"You're one to talk."

They shared a grin.

"I know. That's one thing I've discovered about myself since the accident. I think I've been terribly spoiled all my life."

"Maybe. But I would never've guessed you were James Adkins's daughter. You never acted stuck-up with me."

The waiter arrived with their menus and they paused to read them.

"What's good here?" she asked as she scanned the list.

"You don't remember?"

She lifted her gaze to his to discover the look she hated. The look that asked for the thousandth time if her memory had come back.

"Please, Max. Don't look at me like that."

"Like what?"

"You're wondering if I remember something, but I don't. And I hate that look. It's like I'm standing in the middle of the room in my underwear while everyone else is fully clothed."

Max's grin lit up his blue eyes.

"That's an interesting analogy."

She didn't think she was a person to blush often, but the mental picture brought heat to her cheeks. "I—I—"

"We'd better figure out what we're going to order. The waiter's on his way over here," he said, changing gears.

"Did we come here before?"

"All the time."

"What did I order?"

Max explained about all her favorites and they ordered. As soon as the waiter left the table, she drew a deep breath and began the question that had been bothering her for days.

"Max, how—"

"How did we meet?"

"No. Yes. Okay, how did we meet?" That wasn't the question she had in mind, but maybe it would be better to wade into these murky waters rather than dive in over her head. After all, they had all evening.

"You came into the model home I have. I happened to be there. We started talking and you told me you were an interior designer, looking for work."

Caroline frowned, thinking about what he'd said. It made sense, if she'd argued with her father about her future. But somehow, she wasn't satisfied. She shifted on the booth seat and brushed her leg against his. Immediately her pulse picked up speed.

"Something wrong?"

"No. I just—nothing." How could she explain that his slightest touch filled her with all kinds of fantasies? "What happened then?"

He didn't answer right away. She frowned, wondering why he was hesitating, when he reached over and took her hand. Raising it to his lips, he caressed it and then laid their clasped hands across his thigh.

"Nothing the hell should've happened, but I couldn't let you walk away. I hate to admit it, but you knocked me for a loop."

"I did?" She wanted to run her hand up and down his thigh, to feel his muscles tense under her touch. Instead, she let her hand rest in his, hoping he wouldn't notice her palm was sticky with desire. "Did you ask me out?"

He chuckled and she was amazed to see the blood surge beneath his tanned cheeks as he looked away.

"I did," he said and then added, "once I got up my courage."

She pulled her hand from his and grasped his chin to bring his face around to hers. "Wait a minute, Max, I may be gullible, but let's not take this to the ridiculous."

"What?"

"You were afraid to ask me out? I bet you have to beat off the women with a stick, so don't give me this shy bit."

He leaned toward her until their mouths were only inches apart, and said, "None of them ever meant anything to me. You did."

She gulped, her heart fluttering wildly. "Even then?"

"Then, now and always," he whispered, and his lips reached for hers.

"Good evening."

As absorbed as they were in each other, Caroline and Max hadn't noticed Prescott's approach. Without waiting for an invitation, he slid into the empty side of the booth.

"I hope you don't mind if I join you."

"But we do," Caroline said, her voice stiff.

"Well, if you feel that way, I suppose I could leave, but all the tables are full. When I saw the two of you, I thought maybe you wouldn't mind if I sat with you. I've been on the road all day and it's almost an hour's drive home."

Caroline wasn't sure she believed him, but after exchanging a glance with Max, she nodded. "I suppose—"

"Thanks. Have you already ordered?"

After the waiter was summoned and Prescott placed his order, he turned to the two of them, eagerness on his face.

"What are you two doing? Having a secret rendez-vous? That doesn't seem fair to me and Adrian."

"You and Adrian can—" she began, heat in her voice, when Max intervened, squeezing her hand under the table.

"Have you been working out of town today, Prescott? Just what kind of work do you do for James?"

Max's conversational gambit was far more success-ful than her anger. Prescott explained his responsibili-ties in great detail. Gruesome detail, Caroline thought. She really didn't care what Prescott did for her father.

Now if it had been Max explaining his job, she would've hung on his every word. As it was, she could only admire his skillful handling of Prescott. Before long, Prescott would think he and Max were best friends.

"I do most of the traveling for James. He doesn't like to go out of town as much as he used to. I scout the properties and make reports to him. When he's favor-ably impressed with something, he may take a trip to look at it himself. He, of course, makes the final deci-sion, but he relies heavily on my expertise."

Caroline felt an urge to yawn, but the waiter's arri-val saved her. He delivered plates of steaming pasta that made her mouth water. At least she would have some-thing to do besides listen to Prescott.

Conversation floundered for a few minutes as they each enjoyed the meal. It seemed ages to Caroline since she'd shared lunch at the home. And it hadn't compared to what she was eating now.

Once her hunger was satisfied, Caroline paid more attention to the press of Max's thigh against hers, the strength of his shoulder as she leaned against him. He may have thought she knocked him for a loop, but Caroline had a suspicion the feeling had been mutual.

The question she'd intended to ask at once when he'd thought she wanted to know how they met was much more to the point. And she hoped she got an answer tonight.

And then again, maybe she didn't want to know.

But, she had to.

She had to know how soon they'd made love... and how often. She just hadn't realized how difficult that question would be. None of the men had offered the information.

It might go a long way in informing her just what kind of a woman she was. And if she was sleeping with three men at the same time, she had a lot of room for improvement.

Max, too, had finished eating. He spoke to Prescott again.

"Who supervises out-of-town projects? I should think that would be a lot of hard work. James wouldn't want just anyone to handle that."

Caroline frowned at the man beside her. He was buttering up Prescott as if he were a fat turkey, going into the oven for Thanksgiving. Why? What was he wanting?

"Usually, I'm the one who oversees those projects. James knows he can trust me. I've worked for him for eight years now," Prescott boasted. "And I can tell you he doesn't keep people around if they don't pull their weight. Right, Caroline?"

"Of course," Caroline agreed politely, but she rolled her eyes in disgust. How was she supposed to know? She couldn't even remember past four days ago.

"What are the recent projects you've been working on? Obviously you don't have one going right now."

"Aha. You're hoping to get some investment ideas from me, aren't you? I'll admit everyone wants to follow James. He is a genius."

Max shrugged his shoulders with a grin. "Okay, you caught me. Tell me about some of your past projects, then, if you won't talk about future ones."

Caroline frowned again. Max was up to something, but she couldn't figure out what. Maybe that was because she was too busy watching him, loving the expressions on his face, the grooves down his cheeks, showing how often he smiled. His blue eyes twinkled in the soft light, and she wanted all his attention on her, not Prescott and his boring conversation.

She almost jumped as his hand sought hers under the table. When his warmth flowed into her fingers, she relaxed again and leaned against him.

"Well, last year..." Prescott began, and Caroline almost groaned. The silly man was going to explain in incredible detail every project he'd overseen.

"If you'll excuse me, I'll be right back," she said, interrupting his nonstop spiel.

"Yeah, hurry back," Max whispered as he stood. She looked at him with a frown, but he didn't elaborate.

Was he afraid she'd miss a single second of Prescott's career?

She really did hurry, much to her own surprise, but Max's words intrigued her. Had he discovered something about Prescott? Other than that he liked to talk about himself, of course. That's wasn't a difficult discovery.

She returned to the table, lipstick replaced and her hair combed, just as Prescott began to talk about this year's projects.

When Max took her hand in his again, she was content to sip her tea and wait Prescott out.

"Last June, we started building apartments in Cheyenne, Wyoming. James decided that that city is hitting a growth spurt."

"Cheyenne? Now that interests me," Max said, leaning forward. "How many units did you build?"

Prescott tossed out numbers and Max nodded his head. Caroline wiggled her toes, wishing she and Max were somewhere alone.

"How long did it take to build them?" Max asked.

"Oh, we had a tight deadline on that one. You wouldn't believe how quickly we put those up. Quality building, you understand. We don't skimp on anything. But we finished those apartments in six weeks. Worked straight through the weekends. I didn't get home the entire time," Prescott said, leaning back, as if waiting for accolades for his dedication.

Max squeezed Caroline's hand, but she'd already caught the significance of Prescott's words.

"You stayed there the entire time, Prescott? What dedication."

"Oh, I'm glad to do it, Caroline. Your dad's a terrific man to work for."

"Yes, but I do have one question."

"Sure. Ask anything you like."

His expansive mood almost made Caroline feel sorry for him.

Almost.

"Just how did you manage to get me pregnant if you weren't even here for six weeks?"

Chapter Seven

Prescott had leaned back against the cushion of the booth, his glass in hand, taking a sip of the red wine he'd ordered to accompany the pasta. Quite the sophisticated diner.

With Caroline's question, he almost jackknifed into his plate, sputtering wine everywhere.

"I—we—you—"

"*We* didn't do anything... together, that is," Caroline assured him. Even if he didn't admit he'd lied, after his reaction, she felt confident that he had. "So now I'd like you to explain why you claimed to be the father of my baby."

"You visited me!" Prescott gasped, his last-ditch effort undermined by his pale cheeks.

"Give it up, man," Max advised, a grim smile on his face.

Slumping back against the cushions again, Prescott sighed and avoided Caroline's gaze. "Okay. I lied."

"Yes, but why?" She leaned forward, eager for his response.

"Look, Caroline, I've always admired you. You weren't interested, I knew that. But you were in trouble, and...and it wouldn't hurt me in your dad's eyes if I helped you out."

"Helped me out?" Caroline gasped. "Don't you think claiming to have fathered my baby goes a little beyond 'helping me out'?"

"Maybe," Prescott admitted, "but I had good intentions."

"What about the other guy?" Max asked.

Prescott's eyes narrowed and he asked cautiously, "You mean Adrian?"

"Have there been any others claiming my baby?" Caroline asked in exasperation.

"I don't know anything about Adrian and you. The two of you have gone out, like us, but mostly to social events your father or your mother insisted you attend."

"Where was he the end of June?"

"I don't know, Caroline, really, I don't. I worked my tail off on that project. Your dad's getting ready to make a decision about which one of us will be promoted to second in command. I thought I could sway his decision by bringing that project in on time."

"It sounds like a good plan to me," Max murmured.

"If you think efficiency would win out over a son-in-law, the father of his grandchild, I've got some swampland in Florida to sell you," Prescott said.

"Good point," Max agreed with a rueful grin.

Caroline stared at the two of them. "Great! Just great! I'm being discussed like a fringe benefit and you two are bonding! Men!"

Both of them hurried to assure her that they would never think of her as a Christmas bonus or a three-day weekend, at least that was her interpretation of their protestations, but Caroline had heard enough.

"I have a headache," she announced, and asked Max to let her out of the booth.

"Where are you going?"

"Home."

"You came in a taxi. I'll take you home."

"I can take her home. I live near her parents' house," Prescott assured Max. "It'll save you a long drive."

"I don't mind."

"You don't have to worry about me chasing after her now. She probably won't speak to me after tonight."

"Naw, she wouldn't hold a grudge that long."

"Excuse me," Caroline raged. "Why don't you two gentlemen flip a coin while I go powder my nose."

She really only intended to powder her nose, but as she reached the lobby of the restaurant, she saw a couple just exiting a taxi. It took only a minute to take their place. With a message to be delivered by the maître d', along with a healthy tip, she climbed into the taxi, gave her address and leaned back, closing her eyes.

She'd tried to do too much so soon after her accident. But at least she'd eliminated one suitor. Now if she could just find a way to get rid of Adrian.

And then she could decide what to do about Max.

"Sir, the lady said to tell you that she took a taxi."

"How did she find a taxi so quickly?" Max asked, staring at the maître d'.

"Some customers were arriving in one and she took it."

Max thanked the man for delivering the message and settled back with a frown.

"That's Caroline for you," Prescott muttered. "She's always been damned independent. She drives her father crazy."

"I can believe that, but I'm not her father, and it's about time she learned that." Max reached for his back pocket.

"What are you going to do?"

"I'm going to see Caroline home."

"But she just left."

"Uh-uh." Max signaled to the waiter. "By the way, you didn't turn up here accidentally, did you?"

"No. I was waiting for Caroline when the chauffeur returned, and he told me where you were."

"I thought as much." When he pulled out his credit card, Prescott stopped him.

"I'll take care of the bill, Max. After all, I horned in on the two of you. Go ahead and do whatever you're going to do. I wish you luck."

"Thanks," Max said, shaking Prescott's hand.

Then he was up and out of there, in pursuit of a very stubborn lady. He was determined to beat her to her house. If he didn't, he was afraid she wouldn't see him.

Once he turned off the freeway, he kept his eyes open for a taxi. When he spotted one just a block ahead of him, he breathed a sigh of relief.

He passed the taxi about two blocks before Caroline's house. In the darkness, he could see only one passenger. He hoped it was Caroline. Pulling into the driveway, he pressed the button, hoping someone would let him in.

"Yes?"

"Mrs. Lamb? This is Max Daniels. Caroline is on her way home and I'd like to come in and wait for her."

"Of course, Mr. Daniels."

Without any more conversation, the big gates swung open. He hadn't expected it to be that easy. When he stopped his car in front of the door, he got out and leaned against it, waiting for Caroline. He didn't want to wait inside.

And all the while, he worried that the taxi he'd seen might not have been Caroline's. He was going to feel pretty dumb if she didn't come home.

Two minutes later, he heard the gates swing open again. Tensing, he watched as the taxi pulled to a stop beside his car. He swung open the taxi door as Caroline was paying the fee. She gasped, obviously not having noticed that he was there.

"What are you doing here?"

"Waiting for you."

The taxi driver looked from him to Caroline. "Lady, if there's a problem, I can call the cops."

She shook her head, much to Max's relief. "No, that's not necessary."

Caroline got out of the taxi, after giving the driver what must have been a generous tip, from the delight on his face, and they both stood silently, watching the taxi depart. Then she faced him, her chin tilted at its most stubborn angle.

"Why did you follow me?"

"I don't think you can call it following since I got here first," he said, glaring at her.

She stamped her foot. "Max! Why are you here?"

"Because something I was about to do got interrupted, and I refuse to be put off any longer." He didn't wait to see if she asked for an explanation. He was tired of waiting. Tired of being interrupted. And most tired of not touching her. As she opened her mouth to protest, he pulled her into his arms and lowered his lips to hers.

The magic that always filled him at her touch returned full force. All he could think about was her. His hands caressed her back, circling her slim form while his mouth held hers captive.

When he finally came up for air, he muttered, as if in explanation so she wouldn't know how much she affected him, "I don't like my dates running out on me."

She tried to pull away but he held her tighter. "You're not going anywhere, Caroline, until you promise to stop doing that."

"I only did it once, Max. I don't think you could call that a habit," she protested.

Her body pressed against his made it hard to think, but he reminded her, "You ran out on me the morning after we made love."

"We only made love once?"

"Yeah." Though he'd planned on many more nights spent with her in his arms.

"Why?"

"Why what?"

"Why did we only make love once? Didn't you want to again?"

There was a quaver in her voice that almost brought him to his knees. She had no idea how much she affected him. Gruffly he replied, "I told you. You ran out on me."

As she stared up at him, her gaze puzzled, one hand slipped up his chest to caress the nape of his neck. Shivers ran down his spine and he tightened his hold on her as his lips took hers again.

"Max!" Caroline protested when he released her at last. "You—you shouldn't—"

"Yes, I should. I should take you to my bed and never let you out of it," he growled.

Before he could kiss her again, she put her hand between their lips. "But Max, why did I leave?"

"I don't know, damn it!" Frustration filled him for several different reasons. "I didn't know why, and I couldn't find you. I still don't know why. But at least I know where to find you." And he showed her by claiming her lips again. As his hands caressed her, they encountered the buttons on her blouse. Though Max would have liked nothing better than to strip naked on the spot, both of them, some remnant of sanity, or the cool night air on her skin made Caroline corral his searching fingers.

"Max," she protested, breaking off their kiss, "Let's go inside." Slowly she pulled away from him, the clouds of passion gradually clearing in her eyes.

"Inside?" he asked, his desire unabated.

"Yes, come inside, Max." She took out her key and opened the front door. Mrs. Lamb appeared in the hallway only seconds after. "It's only me, Mrs. Lamb, with Max. We're—we're going to talk a little in the sun room."

Talk wasn't what he was interested in. He followed her into the sun room, wondering if she would let him touch her again. He felt like a starving man having only had his hunger aroused after ignoring it for too long. He needed to touch her again.

Much to his delight, she turned into his arms as soon as he closed the door behind them.

"Max, this feels so right. I can't—I don't want to hold back."

"You won't get any argument from me, sweetheart," he assured her as he held her against him. "No argument at all."

Just as he was lowering his lips to hers, however, she said, "I wish it had been more than once."

Max froze, puzzling over her words. When he could make no sense out of them, he asked, "Why?"

"Because it might explain why I ran away." She backed away from him, as if she feared his nearness would undermine her resolve.

"What are you talking about?" he asked as he followed her.

"Think about it, Max. It's obvious I—I'm attracted to you. I can hardly keep my hands off you. Why would I run away from that?" She didn't wait for an answer, assuming he had one. "But if I'd had a fight with, say, Adrian, and run away, I might have felt that I'd betrayed him when you and I—when we—"

Max eliminated the distance between them in a flash and drew her against him again. "No! Look, we didn't just meet one day and fall into bed! That's not how I operate!"

"I don't think it's how I operate, either," Caroline said with a rueful laugh, "but I can't remember."

"Well, I can. And I know a classy lady when I see one," he added, his lips caressing hers again. He almost lost track of what he'd been going to say as remembered sensations filled him. Making love to Caroline had been like nothing he'd experienced before.

He broke off the kiss to continue before it was too late. "When I met you, you didn't come on to me, or even really flirt with me. Not then. We just talked. But there was something between us, some spark, or pull. I can't explain it, but I've never felt it before."

"Well, obviously, we're sexually compatible," Caroline offered, laying her head on his shoulder.

"I've been sexually compatible before," he said dryly, and felt her tense up against him.

"With whom?" she demanded, a fierce frown on her face.

He dropped a quick kiss onto her lips and stepped away. "No one you'd know, but I'm thirty-four. Did you expect me to be a virgin?"

"Isn't that what men always want? Why can't I want the same thing?"

"You can, but you won't get it with me. Besides, that's a little unreasonable since you're the one with three men claiming your baby."

"Prescott lied," she hurriedly said.

"And Adrian?"

She turned away from him. "I don't know. I worry about it all the time." Turning to face him, she said, "That's why I thought—it would've been better if we'd had a—a relationship, not a one-night stand."

"Wait a minute, lady. It wasn't a one-night stand."

"Why not? It only happened once, you said. It was at night, wasn't it?" Though she was smiling, there was a worried look in her eyes that moved him.

"Do you always take things this literally?" he teased, stepping to her side and rubbing her shoulders. "It wasn't a one-night stand, at least on my part, because if I'd had a choice, I would never have let you out of my bed again."

"Never? You must have incredible stamina," she said, smiling at him even as she wrapped her arms around his neck, inviting his kiss again.

Max more than met her halfway, putting aside any idea of discussing their past. She was in his arms again and he never wanted to let her go.

She broke away from him. "Max, did—did you think about a future? For us, I mean?"

"Hell, yes! I told you I didn't ever intend to let you go."

"No, you said you didn't intend to let me out of your bed. That's a little different from what I'm asking," she pointed out ruefully.

"You're asking if I had honorable intentions?" He pulled her closer to him again. "Yeah, I did. I didn't want to rush you, but I had every intention of marrying you."

"But you've never married before?"

"Nope."

"Why? Don't you want a family?"

"I want you. And whatever comes with you. And that's the reason I've never married. I never met a woman I couldn't live without. Until I met you."

He saw tears in her eyes and pressed her head against his shoulder. "Don't cry, sweetheart."

"It's okay," she said, her voice muffled. "I didn't even realize I wanted a family until I found out about the baby. But I do. I want a real family, a daddy, too. And, oh, Max, I want that daddy to be you!"

A YEARNING FILLED Caroline, so strong that it almost obliterated any restraint. She wanted to belong to this man, as old-fashioned as that sounded. She also wanted him to belong to her. Something deep within her shouted that he was her perfect mate.

But had she realized that fact before or after she'd slept with another man?

She shoved such destroying thoughts aside. Tonight, she only wanted Max to fill her mind. She wanted—

"Caroline?" Mrs. Lamb called through the door.

Caroline was greatly relieved the housekeeper hadn't entered, since Max was holding her tightly against him and her hair and makeup showed the signs of their embrace.

"Yes, Mrs. Lamb?"

"I just wondered if you two wanted something to snack on?"

"I'm only hungry for you," Max whispered in her ear, a melodramatic leer on his face.

She ignored him. "Thank you, Mrs. Lamb. That would be nice."

"I'll bring a tray, then."

She moved away from Max as Mrs. Lamb's footsteps faded down the hallway.

"Change your mind?"

He'd followed her.

"About what?"

"About us," he reminded her, slipping his arms around her again.

"Not exactly," she said, turning to face him within his embrace. "It's just that—that we have too many questions facing us to just forget about the past."

"I thought that was exactly what you'd done," he reminded her, a grin on his lips.

"Max, be serious. I did, but you know it wasn't on purpose. It's so daunting, having no past, no memories. I think what we've just shared is really special, but how do I know? I have nothing to compare it to."

"Just trust your heart, Caroline. Or trust me. I can assure you it's special."

She played with a button on his shirt, twisting and turning it, trying to figure out how to explain her confusion. He lifted her face up with a determined finger under her chin.

"Well?"

She laid her head on his shoulder. "I want to trust you, Max, but even if what we shared was special, we don't know if I found that out after I got pregnant, or before."

For the first time, *he* moved away from *her*. "Prescott was lying."

"I know, and it's a great relief to have eliminated *someone!* But as much as I want him to be a liar, too, I don't know that Adrian is. Apparently, I did go out with him often. And he seems quite sure that he's the father."

"Doesn't that strike you as weird? That he would be so sure that he's the father? You spent two weeks with me. Didn't he even wonder where you were?"

"I don't know! I've only spoken to him the night you all came to dinner. Last night. I haven't had time to investigate his claim."

"You sound like a damned insurance investigator, Caroline! We're talking about making love!"

"Oh, thanks for telling me. I was confusing being pregnant with a car wreck! Throwing up always does that to me!" She moved across the room, putting more distance between them, glaring at him.

"Caroline, you're not being very—"

Another knock on the door preceded Mrs. Lamb's entrance with a well-filled tray of snacks and drinks. "Here you are. I wasn't sure what Mr. Daniels liked, so I fixed a lot of different things."

Caroline turned with relief to the housekeeper. At least with Mrs. Lamb, everything was straightforward. Not like the maze her emotions were in concerning Max. "Thanks, Lambie. You shouldn't have gone to so much trouble."

"No trouble at all. With your parents at that city council banquet, it's been too quiet here this evening."

"Don't worry about cleaning up. Why don't you take the evening off, since they're gone. I'll bring the tray to the kitchen later."

"That'd be nice, honey, but I'll be available if you need anything." With a nod to Max, the housekeeper left the room.

They stood as if frozen, with Mrs. Lamb's footsteps the only noise. Finally Caroline moved into the role of hostess. "Would you care for something to eat?"

"No."

"Then what do you want, Max?" she asked in frustration.

He stared at her, his gaze both hard and hot, a mixture of determination and desire. "You. I want you, and nothing else."

A part of her responded to his words, wanting to fling herself into his arms and throw care and truth to the winds. A large part of her wanted to do that. But that small nagging conscience kept tugging on her desire, telling her to wait. Damn her conscience.

"Max, until I know the truth about—about the baby, and what I was doing, I can't commit to anything."

"Then let's figure it out, Caroline, because I'm having a hard time holding back."

"You could try cold showers?" she suggested, hoping to lighten the tension as her gaze skimmed his impressive form, one few women would want to resist.

"I'm already a shriveled prune. What more do you want?"

He'd responded with teasing, as she'd offered her suggestion, but now she couldn't joke. "I want you, Max," she whispered. Then, before he could reach her, as he showed every intention of doing, she added, "But I also want, need, the truth."

He had closed the distance between them but he didn't touch her. The two inches between them could have been a mile, filled with frustration and confusion.

Max took a deep breath before saying, "Surely someone knows something, Caroline. We've just got to start asking questions."

"Yes. I've tried, but... but I'll try again. Someone must know something."

At that moment, the door to the sun room burst open and Chelsea, dressed in a silk maternity dress, holding a piece of paper in her hand, entered the room, followed by the faithful Roddy in a tux.

"Caroline, I must speak to—oh. I didn't know you had company. Hello, Mr. Daniels." She waited until Max acknowledged her greeting before saying, "It's just as well you're here, however. Because I have something to say that you both need to hear. We can tell Prescott and Adrian later."

Caroline and Max exchanged startled glances. Did Chelsea hold the key to their puzzle?

Chapter Eight

"What is it?" Caroline gasped, taking a step toward her sister. "Have you remembered something?"

"Remembered something? What are you talking about?" Chelsea demanded, staring at Caroline as if she were crazy. Roddy, meanwhile, had wandered over to the tray and was sampling the snacks.

"About my amnesia. About what happened two months ago," Caroline explained, her gaze glued to her sister.

"Don't be ridiculous. I told you I didn't remember anything. I want to talk to you about names." Chelsea moved over to the sofa and sat down. "Roddy, come sit with me."

As Chelsea's husband reluctantly followed her orders, Caroline exchanged a confused look with Max before she too sat down. She didn't think her shaky knees would hold her up much longer. "What are you talking about, Chelsea?"

"Names! Now, don't tell me you haven't been thinking about them. Why, that's the first thing I considered." She spread out the piece of paper on her lap and studied it.

"Names?"

Exasperation filled Chelsea's face. "For the baby, of course. I'm trying to be understanding, Caro. Daddy explained that you hadn't gotten pregnant to upstage me on purpose, so I thought the polite thing to do would be to give you a list of names that you shouldn't consider. That way you won't be disappointed if I select one of them for my baby, who will be born first, of course."

As if that would be a shock for me, Caroline thought. "I know, Chelsea. I can count."

Chelsea sniffed, as if dismissing her sister's sarcasm. "What names have you already thought of?"

The humor of the situation struck Caroline, fortunately, and she leaned back in her chair. "I've been too busy trying to name the daddy, Chelsea. I haven't had time to think about names for the baby."

"Well," Chelsea said, as if instructing the uninformed, "you need to consider them at once. People always ask, and you need an answer ready. Otherwise those questions will keep coming up, again and again."

"Like my breakfast," Caroline muttered. Max gave her a sympathetic smile as he pulled a chair to her side, then clasped her hand as he sat down.

"Caroline! That's most distasteful. You'll ruin Roddy's appetite."

Since Roddy had moved the tray to the coffee table in front of him and his wife and had continued to eat, Caroline wasn't too worried. Roddy, however, with a guilty glance at Chelsea, leaned back, away from the table.

"See? It's okay, Roddy. I'm sure Caroline didn't mean to be so unmannerly." Chelsea returned her attention to her list, and Roddy leaned forward to select another hors d'oeuvre.

"I don't think a week of intestinal flu could ruin his appetite," Max muttered, leaning close to her.

Caroline enjoyed the warmth of his smile as he exchanged looks with her. It made her want to turn into his embrace, to feel the comfort of his arms around her. She wanted to be alone with Max. But that wasn't wise.

"Now, I know it may not seem fair to you since you're the firstborn, but I've put on my list the name Etta Mae." Chelsea challenged Caroline with her gaze.

"Etta Mae?" Max gasped, bending forward in surprise. "Why would she not think it's fair? Why would she even—"

"Max!" Caroline exclaimed, stopping him from expressing his opinion about the name, though she had to struggle to hide her smile. "That's our grandmother's name."

"Oh. Are you disappointed?"

She loved the concern mixed with horror in his voice. He didn't want to hurt her feelings.

"No. That's all right, Chelsea. You can have grandmother's name."

"Well, really, Caroline, how can you just give up so easily? Haven't you thought about it? grandmother's sure to give a handsome gift to the great-grandchild named after her. She might even make special arrangements in her will for her."

Chelsea never noticed the look of amusement that passed from Caroline to Max. He relaxed against the back of the chair as he realized Caroline wasn't like her sister. Unfortunately, he apparently couldn't hold back his feelings.

"You would name a child Etta Mae for money?"

Chelsea glared at him. "An inheritance is important to a child, even if she's too young to realize. Besides, Etta Mae is a charming name. Old-fashioned."

"Definitely," Max agreed gravely, and Caroline covered her lips with her fingers, pretending to cough.

"That's not the only female name I've chosen, though. I might name her after Mother. Amelia is a charming name, also. Mother might even *notice* that she has a grandchild if I did that, instead of always thinking about her charities!"

The plaintive note in Chelsea's voice sounded all too familiar to Caroline, but she couldn't help responding to the need in her sister's voice. "Chelsea, she'll notice your baby. I'm sure she's excited about it."

"No, she's not," Chelsea said bluntly. "A friend called her the other day to discuss giving me a shower and Mother was too busy to talk." She blinked rapidly, as if dismissing tears, before looking at Caroline. "And that's another thing. I'm not sharing a shower with you."

Caroline remembered her first sight of her family. She'd wondered how anyone could love such a strange group. But she felt sorry for Chelsea, craving her mother's attention. Amelia only had eyes for the needy—but she was blind to the fact that her own daughter was one of them.

"That's all right. I'm not ready for a shower. And Mother won't notice my baby if she doesn't notice yours."

"That's true," Chelsea said, brightening.

Caroline almost chuckled. She guessed misery did love company. At least, Chelsea did.

"Now, the only other girl's name I'm going to reserve is Madonna Louise. That way she would be named after someone important and me, too."

Max erupted into a fit of coughing that tested Caroline's self-control. "I think I prefer Etta Mae," he whispered.

"Roddy, how do you feel about the names?" Caroline asked, curiosity filling her. He had said nothing since they arrived.

"Hmm? Oh, whatever Chelsea wants."

"I see." She carefully avoided Max's gaze, turning back to her sister. "I don't think we have any conflicts with those names."

"Oh, good. Now, about the boy's names. He will, of course, be named Roderick Grant IV, but I've put several other names on the list for the future. It's not fair for you to use all the good names just because you don't have a husband to name your baby after."

"Lucky me," Caroline agreed, unable to hold back the grin she sent Max's way. He was silently chuckling, shaking his head back and forth.

She was a little embarrassed at Chelsea's reaction and only hoped Max would understand. It occurred to her to wonder how Max's family would react to their announcement. Assuming, of course, there was anything to announce.

"So, I'm placing dibs on Daddy's name. After all, if I have a second boy, he'll need a good inheritance, too."

"Of course. Umm, what about Roddy's family? Aren't there any wealthy people on his side?"

Chelsea stared at her as if she'd lost her mind. "Don't be ridiculous. You know Roddy's family is one of the wealthiest in the state, along with ours. But I think Daddy should come first, after Roddy and his father. Don't you think so, Roddy?"

Roddy, with his mouth full of a chicken-salad finger sandwich, nodded quickly, muttering what might have been a yes. Caroline wasn't sure.

"Any other names?" Max asked innocently, and Caroline turned to stare at him. "I think Muhammad Ali Grant would be nice."

"Max," Caroline warned even as she grinned.

Chelsea, however, didn't take offense. "You're being frivolous," she said calmly. "We would never give our child an unchristian name, but it is important that they have a name of substance. You'd better think about that when you choose your child's name."

Max looked at Caroline, his gaze suddenly filled with realization, as if it hadn't occurred to him that her pregnancy would result in a baby. But then, he wasn't throwing up every morning.

"I think we still have a little time to decide," Caroline assured both her sister and Max.

"It's best not to wait—"

The opening of the sun room door interrupted Chelsea's warning. Amelia, James and Adrian entered.

"Good evening, children. Mrs. Lamb said you were all here. Any hors d'oeuvres left, Roddy?" James asked, heading for the tray at once.

"Yes, sir. Of course, sir," Roddy hastened to assure his father-in-law, reluctantly pushing the tray to the end of the table near the chair James chose.

"Good. I'm starved. From the meal they served this evening, one would think the city was on the verge of bankruptcy," he grumbled.

"I thought the chicken was delicious," Amelia commented. "I'm sure it had almost no calories, once I removed the skin. You should've followed my advice, James, and removed the skin. You never pay attention to your calorie intake."

While the two older members of the new arrivals were discussing food, Adrian drew a chair next to Caroline's other side and sat down.

"Good evening, Caro. I called earlier to see if you wanted to accompany me to the banquet, but Mrs. Lamb said you were out."

She gave him a brief smile. "Yes. Thank you for thinking of me."

He lifted her hand from the arm of the chair and drew it to his lips for a brief caress. Max was still holding her other hand and she could feel the tension emanating from his body.

"I always think about you, my dear. After all, we're going to be married."

His assumption set up her back, but it also disturbed her deep within. He sounded so confident. And he wasn't her choice.

"I'm not as sure about that as you are, Adrian. I don't think we've had a chance to discuss why you think you're the father of my child." She pulled her hand free, putting it in her lap, as far away from him as possible.

"Do you really want to discuss our affair here? In front of everyone? That's why I've kept quiet about it, of course, because you didn't want your father to know."

His words had such a ring of truth to them that she almost gasped. Of course she wouldn't want her father to know. Could she have been having an affair with Adrian before she met Max?

"If that's true, why did I go away for two weeks without telling anyone where I was going?"

Adrian's possessive gaze shifted from Caroline to Max and back again. "Is that what he told you?"

"That's what Mrs. Lamb told me, and Lewis, and my father and mother."

"Ah, but you didn't keep it a secret from everyone. *I* knew where you were going."

"I don't believe you," she whispered, panic filling her voice.

"I knew where you were going because you were going away with me. And that's why you didn't tell anyone. The secret, remember?" He leaned closer and smiled.

"That's a lie!" Max exclaimed, leaping up from his chair.

"Caroline knows it's the truth," Adrian said, standing to stare at Max.

Caroline, confused but worried Max might throw a punch at Adrian, stood also. "I—I don't know that! I can't remember anything!"

"What's going on?" James demanded, his interest drawn from the food.

"I was just explaining to this gentleman that I'm the father of Caro's baby," Adrian said, nodding at his employer.

"Great! Then we can get on with the wedding plans," James said, clapping his hands with pleasure. "I want a wedding right away. People will count, of course, when the baby is born, but the sooner the better."

"It's not that simple," Caroline exclaimed.

"You promised you'd marry the father of the baby, Caro," James reminded her.

"Yes, but Adrian has offered no proof that he's the father of my child." She turned to face Adrian and felt Max's hands come to rest on her shoulders as he stood behind her. "Do you have proof, Adrian?"

"I have plane tickets to Las Vegas for the day you left home, returning two weeks later."

"Do either of them have my name on them?"

"No, just my name and companion," he said, smiling a rueful grin. "Secrecy, remember?"

"I think I'm going to hate that word the rest of my life," Caroline muttered.

"You could've been accompanied by anyone," Max growled.

"Yes, I could've, but I wasn't. I was accompanied by Caroline. We've been, uh, dating about four months now. But she didn't want her father to know we were involved. She said he'd put too much pressure on her to marry."

"Damn right," James agreed.

"It's too late now, darling," Adrian assured her, taking both her hands in his. "The baby makes things too complicated for me to keep silent." His voice was filled with seeming concern and love.

With Max clasping her shoulders and Adrian her hands, Caroline felt torn in two. She didn't want Adrian to be the father of her baby. But wanting didn't make something so. The feelings he expressed touched her, even if she didn't want to hear them. Who was telling the truth?

"This is too frustrating! Why can't I remember?"

"You probably weren't getting enough vitamin B-6," Amelia murmured. "Or was it B-12? Or maybe another number, I'm not sure. But I was reading that it could improve your memory. I'll look for the article tomorrow."

Caroline pulled away from the two men's touch. "Mother, I have amnesia from a bump on the head, not from something I ate." She turned around to see both Adrian and Max staring at her.

"I need proof. My memory isn't going to work for me, so I have to have proof." She looked at Max. "Do you have anything to show me that I spent those two weeks with you?"

He stared at her, and she wished she could read his mind. "Only this," he said quietly before closing the distance between them. Without another word, he pulled her against him and kissed her.

Caroline distantly heard gasps of outrage behind her, but she was too caught up in the senses Max inflamed. The man's touch was devastating.

He released her and stepped back. "I have no proof, sweetheart, except that we had something special."

Adrian stepped forward. "Anyone can kiss a lady," he said dryly. "Shall I demonstrate?"

Caroline moved away to stand behind her mother's chair. "No...no, I realize that isn't exactly proof." But Max had a point. His kisses were incredible. "Max, didn't you introduce me to anyone? Or—"

"What would that prove? I could bribe half a dozen people to swear they met you, but so could Adrian." Max was staring at her, tension on his face, but Caroline glanced at Adrian as Max spoke. There was an acknowledgment in his face, as if that had already occurred to him.

"True," she agreed, studying the two men consideringly. How could she figure out who was telling the truth?

Finally she faced her father. "Daddy, until someone offers me proof, I refuse to marry. If you're going to be embarrassed by the presence of an unwed pregnant daughter in your house, I'll move out."

"You'll do no such thing!" James exclaimed. "No one will criticize *my* daughter. But I'd rather you marry."

"We just had Chelsea's wedding last year," Amelia said. "I really think it would be better to wait another year for Caroline's. I told her she should've married before Chelsea, but she wouldn't listen to me."

"Amelia," James answered with open impatience, "if we wait a year for Caroline's wedding, the baby will have already been born. Your grandchild will be illegitimate. I can assure you that is more socially unacceptable than having two weddings within a year of each other."

"But, James, it would take at least a year to even plan a wedding." She peered around her distraught husband to stare accusingly at Caroline. "You should have given me at least a year's notice, dear."

Hysterical laughter bubbled up in Caroline. Of course, she should've planned her pregnancy, and, for that matter, her amnesia, better, for her mother's sake. In fact, as long as she was planning, she should've left a note with the name of the daddy. It would've saved her a lot of trouble.

"I'm sorry, Mother, but I didn't exactly plan what has happened. *If* I marry, I think we can keep it simple and not need a year's preparation."

"Of course you'll marry," James ordered.

"To me," Adrian added.

His insistence was getting on her nerves. "Not without proof," she reminded him coolly.

"I'll get proof."

She turned her gaze to Max, trying not to plead with her eyes. She wanted him to assure her that he, too, would offer proof. That he was, indeed, the father of her child. That he loved her.

That thought hit her like a punch in the stomach. Loved her? Was she in love with Max? Of course she was if she went to bed with him, she assured herself. But did she? Or had she been sleeping with Adrian? Was she the kind of person who slept with a man because her hormones were in overdrive? And was Adrian a person who could arouse those hormones? She didn't have any doubt about Max's abilities in that area.

"I'm tired. It's been a long day."

"But I haven't explained about the names to Adrian," Chelsea suddenly said, having silently watched the drama unfold. "After all, it appears that he'll have more to say about it than Mr. Daniels."

"No, Chelsea. I'll decide the name of my child, or at least, I will until I'm sure who the daddy is."

"But he just said—" Chelsea began.

"I know what he said! That doesn't make it truth. Until I have proof, this is my child, and mine alone."

"I don't think that's physically possible, dear," Amelia murmured, staring at her daughter.

Caroline wondered if her mother could possibly be insane, but there was a twinkle in her mother's gaze that sent a sigh of relief through her. "No, probably not, Mother, but I'm beginning to wonder if it wouldn't be easier that way. Maybe I should discuss the topic in my prayers this evening."

"You could try," Amelia said, her voice filled with doubt, "but I've tried it before and nothing changed."

Chapter Nine

If they could put a man on the moon, the least they could do for women was find a way to eliminate morning sickness.

Or make pregnancy possible for men.

After starting the next day by throwing up anything she had consumed in the past century, that was the only thought that made Caroline laugh.

And also made her wonder if part of her sickness was caused by stress.

Why should she be stressed? Just because she had no memory of her life until five days ago, she was pregnant with a baby she had no memory of conceiving, and there were two men who wanted to claim that baby, she had no reason for stress. She groaned and staggered back to her bed just as someone knocked softly on her door.

"Oh, you're already up," Mrs. Lamb said as she entered to Caroline's call to come in, carrying a tray. "Here's some crackers to eat. They'll settle your stomach. I meant to bring them up last night so you'd have them first thing this morning."

"Do they really work?" Caroline asked, finding the idea of eating anything terribly unappealing.

"Most of the time. Have you already been sick?"

"Yes. Over and over again."

"Oh, my stars. You poor thing. Try a cracker and the carbonated water I brought. You're supposed to eat them when you first awake, before you even sit up."

Caroline lay on a pillow, munching crackers and sipping the water while Mrs. Lamb sat on the edge of the bed, watching. Much to Caroline's surprise, her stomach began to return to normal.

"It works, Lambie. I think I may survive."

"Of course you will. You always manage."

Caroline's mood darkened. "Do I? I don't seem to be doing a good job of managing my life right now."

"It's not your fault you got amnesia."

"No, but it's my fault I'm pregnant. At least I think it is. I can't believe I didn't insist on precautions."

Mrs. Lamb's cheeks flushed red, but she looked right at Caroline. "Even without a memory, I'm sure you know that sometimes a woman can be swept away by—by passion."

Caroline smiled at her. Clearly embarrassed, the older woman still had said what she felt needed to be said. As if it would—her thoughts skidded to a halt.

"Wait a minute, Lambie, I think you've got a point."

"Well, of course I do."

Sitting up, Caroline took the housekeeper's hand. "No, I don't mean—I mean, you may have found a clue about who's the daddy of my baby."

"I did? What clue?"

"If I was so swept away by passion that I didn't think of protection, which of the two men could arouse such forgetfulness?" She grinned because she already knew the answer and she liked it—a lot.

"Two? I thought there were three?"

"No, we eliminated Prescott last night. He was lying. Just as one of the others is lying." To be fair, Caroline forced herself to consider Adrian and whether she might be swayed by him. She didn't have to give such thought to Max. Even being in the same room with him accelerated her pulse.

"Are you sure it will be so simple?"

Caroline stared at Mrs. Lamb. Talk about a bucket of cold water. "What do you mean?"

"Maybe you wanted to get pregnant on purpose?"

"Why would I want to do that? Especially if I knew anything about it. Throwing up isn't a lot of fun." She rubbed her unruly stomach.

"That will pass. And you've always been the leader, between you and Chelsea."

Caroline stared at her in horror. "You think I might have wanted to get pregnant—without marrying—to show up my sister?" Mrs. Lamb wasn't painting a very pretty picture of her behavior.

"I didn't say that. I just thought you should consider everything . . . with so much at stake." Mrs. Lamb wasn't meeting her gaze.

"Lambie," Caroline began, reaching out to take the lady's hand, "was I really so spoiled that I would do such a thing?"

"No, not spoiled. I don't know. I just know that Chelsea always thought she had to compete with you. It might be natural for you to respond."

"I think I like your first theory better. I can believe that M—that a man might have swept me off my feet."

"So you think you know which one it is?"

"I hope so. And I'm determined to prove it. I'm tired of sitting around waiting to get back my memory. The doctor said it might be months . . . or never." She threw off the covers and slid from the bed.

"I'll go down and make you some breakfast, then."

Caroline started to protest but was surprised to discover that her stomach seemed to like the idea. Contrary thing! "Okay, but not too much."

Standing under the steamy spray a minute later, she thought about her hastily formed plan. It probably had all kinds of holes in it, but it appealed to her. She was going to get Max to retrace their steps for her. Maybe, just maybe, things she had seen only during those two weeks would bring back the memory she needed.

If it didn't, at least she would get to spend time with Max.

"BOY, ARE YOU A GROUCH this morning," Susan complained.

Max glared at her. "Just get me that file."

She returned in less than a minute, a file in her hand. "Here it is. So, what's bothering you?"

"Nothing."

"I didn't say anything to Mom or Karen about your girlfriend. If they found out, it wasn't from me."

"They didn't find out."

"Oh."

He pretended to study the file he'd asked for, hoping his little sister would take the hint. She didn't.

"So, are you still seeing her?"

"I don't know."

"Did she dump you?" Susan asked in astonishment.

"Susan," he warned, putting every threat he'd ever made toward her—and that covered a lot of territory—into his tone.

"Okay, okay, I'm going, but she's the one who made a mistake, if she did. You're one terrific guy, big brother."

Max held his sigh until she'd closed the door behind her. Sweet of her to try to make him feel better. But it didn't do much good. He *knew* he was the father to Caroline's baby.

But he couldn't prove it.

Without proof, things were at a stalemate.

And he didn't trust Adrian. The man might produce some kind of proof. Some kind of fake proof.

If the man had said he and Caroline had had an affair and then argued, causing her to run away, and Max had caught her on the rebound, he might have believed him. Caroline had been—not upset—but very cautious. Yes, that was the word, cautious.

But Adrian had chosen to lie about those two weeks. So Max knew Adrian wasn't the father of the baby.

The baby was Max's.

He was going to be a daddy.

He'd always intended to have a child, children. Somehow, it had never happened. Shrugging his shoulders, he admitted to himself that he hadn't made much effort.

But when Caroline had walked through the door to the model home, he'd known, as sure as he knew his own name, that she was the one. And while he wouldn't choose to marry her with a child already on the way, he didn't have a problem with becoming a father.

Did he want a boy or a girl? The sex of his child hadn't concerned him, but now he pictured Caroline holding their baby and somehow he just knew she'd be a girl. A baby daughter, just as beautiful as her mother. He'd teach her lots of things. How to defend herself. How to run a business. How to— He smiled even more. He wouldn't have to teach her how to flirt. Her mother would take care of that. Or how to knock a guy off his feet.

Yeah, his baby girl would be perfect. Just like her mother. And he couldn't wait to hold her.

He was lost in thought, contemplating the child, when Susan opened his door.

"Max, I'm going to go to lunch a little early, okay?"

"Yeah." Whatever. He didn't care what she did as long as she didn't ask any more questions about Caroline. She withdrew from the doorway but didn't close his door, so he had no difficulty hearing the outside door open.

"Hello. May I help you?"

"I'm Caroline Adkins. I'm here to see Max Daniels if he's available."

He leaped from his desk at the first word, knowing immediately who had arrived. By the time she finished her request, he was at Susan's side.

"Caroline," he said, trying to control his breathing. He didn't want to sound like an eager puppy.

"You're Caroline?" Susan asked, a smile breaking across her face. "I'm Susan, Max's sister."

"I'm delighted to meet you, Susan," Caroline said, smiling back at her. "I don't know if Max told you, but I have amnesia, so if we've met before—"

"No, we haven't. Max has kept you a secret."

"Oh."

He watched in frustration as disappointment filled her eyes.

"Come into my office, Caroline," he suggested, eager to get her away from his sister before Susan said something she shouldn't. "You can go to lunch, Susan."

"Oh, I'm in no hurry if you need me to do anything," Susan offered, smiling at Caroline.

"No. Go to lunch."

"Okay, okay. Nice to have met you, Caroline."

"Yes. I'm glad to have met you, too."

He slammed the door in the face of their niceties. He was too upset to tolerate them.

"Well, really, Max, what will Susan think?"

"She's already told me what she thinks, several times today. Do you want the exact words?"

He regretted his outburst as Caroline's eyes widened.

"Sorry. I seem to be in a rotten mood this morning."

"Is this the first time you've been angry with me, or have I forgotten the others?"

She tilted her head to one side, waiting for his response, and he wanted to close the distance between them and kiss her until she forgot everything but their passion.

"The only time I really got angry with you was when you walked out on me. And you weren't there to see it."

Caroline stepped away from him, moving over to the window behind his desk. "I know. I wish I could explain—or understand for that matter. And I'm tired of waiting for my memory to come back."

"I don't think you have a lot of choice there," Max replied, his bad humor still in place because of his frustration. When she continued to stare out the window, saying nothing, he asked, "Why are you here?"

She stiffened before turning to face him. "Not interested in company today? Afraid I'll chase away potential customers?"

Though she hadn't answered his question, he played along. "I'm always ready for your company."

Her gaze shifted away from him, making him suspicious. What did she have up her sleeve? And how well did he know her? He'd thought he'd known her, but recent days had proven him wrong.

"Did we come here often?" she abruptly asked, looking around his office.

"Never."

His answer seemed to surprise her. "Why?"

How could she ask such calm questions? Didn't she understand what was at stake? Their future depended on what happened in the next few days. He strode to her side and pulled her into his arms with all the energy of his pent-up frustration. "Because I don't consider this proper business behavior," he muttered before his lips took hers.

Last night had only aroused his passion more, not sated it. He pressed her body against his hardness, his lips insisting that she open to him. He was tired of standing by, waiting for her to acknowledge his role in her life.

"Max!" she gasped, wrenching her lips away. "We can't—"

"Can't what? Make love? We already have. And why the hell you can't remember the magic we make together, I don't know." He'd wasted enough time talking. He'd prove to her that they belonged together in the only way that mattered.

She responded to his kisses, her arms encircling his neck. When he stroked her, she pressed even closer to him, until he thought he'd lose control. Again.

It was the sound of the outside door opening that brought their frantic movements to a sudden stillness.

"Max?"

The masculine voice drew a gasp from Caroline, but Max recognized it at once. He shoved her toward the corner and left her in his office. As he moved, he struggled to button his shirt that had somehow come unbuttoned. "Yeah, Jim?"

"What are you doing? Dressing in the office?" Jim asked, grinning at him.

Max struggled to maintain his cool. "Yeah. What do you need?"

Jim unrolled a house plan and began pointing out some complications to Max. He tried to concentrate on the facts as his body did a slow descent from arousal. It was difficult.

"Well, what do you think?" Jim asked, and stood waiting.

Hell. He had no idea what the man had even asked. Now what was he going to do?

The outer door opened again and Susan walked in.

"I thought you went to lunch?" he growled. He didn't need any more complications.

"I did. I wasn't very hungry." Susan searched the room with her gaze. "Where's Caroline? And why is your shirt buttoned crooked?"

Max looked down at his shirt in embarrassment. Susan was right. He'd buttoned it wrong. He could feel his cheeks flaming.

Jim had never been a slow-top. After another look at the door to Max's office, he grabbed Susan by the arm. "Okay if I take Susan to see the new place?" he asked as he pulled her out the door.

"Great. That'd be great, Jim," Max assured him, silently promising the man a bonus. Intelligence should be rewarded.

Turning to his office, he found Caroline standing in the doorway. He was afraid she'd be angry with what had happened, but she appeared calm. Which was more than he could do.

"They're gone?"

"Yeah."

Without a word, she crossed to him and began unbuttoning his shirt. Before he could misinterpret her movements, she then placed the buttons in the proper holes.

"Thanks," he said huskily, but he couldn't help thinking he would have preferred her to reverse the procedure.

Then she surprised him by saying, "Let's go to your place."

Chapter Ten

Caroline was relieved to get Max behind the wheel of his truck. As long as he was driving, he couldn't distract her with his touch, his kisses. And distraction seemed to come easy for him. But she had some questions she needed answered.

There was no easy way to begin, so she broke their tense silence with the most important one.

"When we made love, why didn't you use protection? Don't you ever—I mean, with other women?"

She watched his hands tighten on the steering wheel, but his response was brief. "Yes."

She stared at him blankly before saying, "Yes, what?"

"Yes, I used protection with other women. I always use protection."

"Not always," she reminded him, several questions still unanswered.

He refused to look at her, keeping his gaze on the road as he swept his hand through his hair. She thought he wasn't going to answer her, but finally he said, "Look, Caroline, when I met you, I—you knocked me off my feet. I wanted to go to bed with you there in the model home where we met." He looked at her with eyes filled with hot passion.

"But we didn't," Caroline said hurriedly, pressing against the truck seat.

"No, we didn't. In fact, even though you were willing to go to dinner with me, you made it damn clear that dinner was all you were offering."

"What happened next?" She knew so little about herself, much less the man next to her. It was like working blindfolded. And she hated it.

"We spent the next two weeks falling in love." He made his blunt statement a challenge, daring her to contradict him.

She drew in a deep breath. "When—when did we—"

"The night before you left."

His responses were more and more brusque. Her inquisition wasn't pleasing him. *Well, too bad,* she thought huffily. She was the one pregnant. She had a right to ask a few questions. Particularly the one he hadn't yet answered.

"Why didn't you use protection?"

"Because I hadn't planned to take you to bed, okay?" he snapped.

"Are you trying to say I seduced you? Or are you blaming me for not having taken care of things, like most men?" She could get just as irritated as him.

"Hell! Caroline, how can you ask such stupid questions? It just happened. Don't you understand how it is between us? I can't touch you without going up in flames. And for your information, lady, you didn't do any holding back yourself."

She looked away, unable to meet his look. How could she argue with him after what nearly happened in his office? Just sitting beside him made her heart pound and her pulse race. "Where were we?"

"We were at my place." He stopped the truck and waved out the windshield with his hand. "Right here."

She ignored his house to finish her questioning. "You didn't have protection here?"

"Damn it, Caroline, what is the point? We didn't use protection. That's pretty obvious since you're pregnant."

"I want to know why."

Staring straight ahead, he said, "Yes, I had protection here. I didn't—hadn't used it in a while, but it was there. I preached too much to my brothers about always being safe not to have some condoms there."

Hadn't he cared enough about her to want to protect her? Was she wrong about him? "Then why?" she whispered.

He whirled in his seat suddenly and seized her by the shoulders. "How many times do I have to tell you? I lose control with you." His lips covered hers again in a demonstration that had her convinced at once.

Knowing she was going under for the count if she didn't do something quickly, Caroline pulled away from him. She clutched the door handle and muttered, "I want to see your house. It looks beautiful."

The glare he shot her didn't show any appreciation, but he wrenched open the door and got out. She quickly followed.

Max's home was his pride and joy. He'd rewarded himself with it a couple of years ago. Set in the foothills of the Rockies, it wasn't huge, with only three bedrooms, but it sported a back porch and patio with a mountain stream nearby.

He opened the front door and stood stiffly aside to let her enter.

"Do you take care of it yourself?" Caroline asked, looking around at the casual furnishings. His sisters had helped with the choices, but he'd made the final decisions, choosing bold, bright colors in comfortable, easy-care fabrics.

"No. The cleaning lady came today, so you shouldn't find any dirty underwear thrown under the bed."

Her eyebrows rose, a smile on her face for the first time since they left the office. "Oh. So that's the kind of person you are."

"I never tried to hide it."

His gruffness washed away her smile. "I know, but since I can't remember anything about those two weeks, it's like I'm meeting you for the first time."

"Not in one way."

"What are you talking about?"

"I'm talking about our bodies, Caroline. Your head may not remember me, but your body does. Surely you can admit that? Or do you want another demonstration?"

She licked her lips and he thought he'd die if he didn't touch her. He stepped forward and then stopped when she moved away from him.

"I want to believe that, Max, but you're a very sexy guy. Maybe you have that effect on every woman you date."

He leaned against the wall, trying to assume a casual pose. "Oh, yeah. You saw the line around the house, didn't you, just waiting to fall into my bed."

She grinned but shrugged her shoulders. "Just because they aren't here at the moment doesn't mean they aren't chasing you."

"Honey, once I met you, I haven't so much as talked to another woman except to order fast food."

She seemed pleased with his words but turned away to look at the living room. He watched her, his hands itching to pull her back into his arms, but he didn't. Things had gotten a little intense, and he didn't want to frighten her away again. "Come on back to the den and I'll fix us a cup of coffee."

She followed him without saying anything.

As they passed the kitchen, Caroline dug in her heels. "Wow. I'm not a great chef, but I know a terrific kitchen when I see one. How perfect, Max."

Memory grabbed him and he blinked several times before explaining. "That's about what you said the first time you saw it."

She gave him a nervous smile and walked into the family room that connected. She moved to the huge windows that looked out toward the stream. "What a marvelous yard for children."

He walked up behind her and slid his hands over her stomach. "Yeah. For my kid." The idea of his being a father was becoming more and more real to him.

Her hands came to rest over his, but when she spoke, he heard the hesitancy in her voice.

"Max, I can't—I don't know."

He tensed again. He hated it when she refused to believe he was the father. When she didn't recognize what they shared. "Caroline, this child is mine. Mine."

"I believe—when you touch me, I have no doubts. It's only afterward, when I think about the past, that I get confused. What if the baby really is Adrian's? What then?"

He clenched his jaw until it ached. "It's not."

"But how can you know? How can any of us be sure until I regain my memory?" With an almost mournful air, she added, "And until I know whose baby this is, I can't make any decisions."

"Then why are we here?" he growled, wanting her, frustrated with her holding back.

"I want to see where we made love."

With his jaw set, he motioned for her to follow him as he led the way up the nearby staircase.

CAROLINE WANTED TO CLOSE her eyes, to run away, rather than face the possibility that this desperate measure wouldn't work. What if there was no recognition? There hadn't been so far.

And Max's house was distinctive, beautiful. She wouldn't forget it, would she?

They reached the top of the stairs with a spacious landing and three doors opening off it. Max led her to the farthest door. He swung it open and stood back for her to enter.

She gasped.

The entire back wall was floor-to-ceiling windows, framing the mountains in awe-inspiring beauty.

"Oh, Max, how stunning!" She turned around to smile at him, thrilled with the beauty of his house. He frowned back at her.

"You don't remember it, do you?"

His flat tones, devoid of emotion, stole her appreciation away. "I want to remember, Max! Truly, I do, but I can't lie to you."

He strode past her to stare out at the mountains. "I never asked you to lie."

"No, just to remember. But I can't do that, either. The doctor said I might never recover my memory."

He spun around to stare at her. "Never?"

She tried to smile as she shrugged her shoulders. "That's what the man said."

Unable to face the despair in his gaze, she moved around the large bedroom, dominated by a king-size bed. The room was decorated in shades of green, touched with rust, a very masculine room. As desperately as she searched for memory of the place, she found none.

He crossed his arms over his chest as he watched her. "Maybe you should look at the ceiling. I don't think you saw much of anything else the last time you were here."

"Max!" she protested automatically as the meaning of his words penetrated. Then a shiver ran over her as her eyes left the ceiling, where she'd automatically looked, to return to him. She could believe his words. Why look at scenery when Max Daniels was available? Only she wanted more than availability. She wanted to awaken every day with Max at her side, to go to sleep each evening in his arms. She wanted his love.

So far, Max had told her he wanted to make love to her, but nothing more. She met his gaze. "It's a wonderful house, Max."

"But you're not here to see my house... or me, are you? You're here to see if you remember anything. Right?" His voice was hard, accusing.

"So what's wrong with that? You want me to get my memory back, don't you?"

"Yeah. But I'd like a little honesty, too. Though that doesn't seem to be your strong suit."

"Max Daniels! How dare you!" It wasn't her fault she couldn't remember what happened.

"How dare I? It's easy, lady. Think about it. Everything you told me was a lie! When I got to that hospital room and found you, I thought I'd found Caroline Adkins, recently arrived from Kansas City, in need of a job, alone in the world. Instead, I find a room full of people, a family with more money than the rest of the state put together, and two other men claiming you."

Her teeth sank into her bottom lip. He was right. She couldn't deny a thing he said. Fighting back the tears, she stared at him, wishing her chin wasn't trembling. "What do you want me to say, Max? I can't remember. I've told you over and over again."

"Just don't say a damn thing," he growled, and turned his back on her.

Wanting to apologize, only she wasn't sure what for, she crossed the room to touch him. It seemed so natural to reach out to him. She wanted to believe she was remembering, but she wasn't sure.

"Don't do that!" Max snapped. "Don't you realize where we are?"

She was beginning to wonder if she'd stumbled into one of those houses of mirrors, where appearances constantly changed. After carefully looking around her, she said, "We're in your bedroom."

"Yeah, my bedroom, where we made love. Are you offering to repeat the experience? I need to know the limits before I kiss you."

Her eyebrows soared in exasperation. "Max! I just wanted to—I don't know what. I don't want to make you angry."

"Are you sure? Or are you still trying to remember?" He reached out and pulled her against him. "Maybe I need to refresh your memory. Do you want to know what really happened the night we made love? Do you, Caroline?"

The anger in his voice should've frightened her. But it didn't. The heat building in her, pooling in her stomach, only made her want his touch more.

"When we made love, I started by kissing you," he muttered, and then did exactly that, covering her lips, taunting her to open them as his tongue sought entrance. After an awe-inspiring kiss, he broke away to say, "Then, I slid my hands down here," and ran his hands down the seat of her pants, caressing her hips, pulling her more tightly against him, letting her feel his arousal.

She gasped and his lips returned to hers, taking the kiss deeper and deeper. One hand left her hip and moved to her breast, caressing it through her blouse.

"Remember?" he whispered before his lips trailed down her throat.

Was she remembering? Or just wanting to remember so badly it felt the same? At that point she didn't much care. She just knew she wanted him.

They were both breathing heavily now. Caroline clung to him as if he were an anchor in a rough sea. His lips trailed his fingers as they began unbuttoning her blouse. When he took her bare breast in his hand, she almost cried out at the exquisite pleasure.

"That's right, Caroline. That's exactly how you reacted. You wanted my touch as much as I wanted to touch you. Do you remember?"

The anger in his voice had gone seductive, purring at her reaction, egging her on. As if she needed it.

She brought his lips back to hers and reached for the buttons of his shirt. His broad chest fascinated her and she wanted to run her hands over him. He was hard and unyielding but warm and inviting, and shivers swept over her.

He began to divest her of all her clothing, muttering as he did so, "At least we have an advantage this time."

She almost didn't hear his comment, as occupied as she was with his magnificent body. "What?"

"I can't get you pregnant."

She gasped, but before she could protest, his lips covered hers again. She gave herself up to the enjoyment they were both experiencing, concentrating on removing Max's clothes as efficiently as he was hers.

In a matter of seconds all restraints were gone, and Max swept her into his arms and carried her to the bed. Caroline didn't know if she remembered his touch or found it so mesmerizing she was confused. She only knew she didn't want him to stop.

As if reading her mind, he said, "Caroline, much farther and I can't stop. Do you want me to stop?" He gasped as he stroked her, caressing her breasts, her hips, every inch of her.

"Oh, no," she pleaded, and sealed his lips with hers. She wanted no more questions. She didn't want to think, only feel. They would be united, as she wanted them to be, forever and ever.

The next few minutes were filled with exquisite sensation. Max anticipated her wants almost before she knew them herself. Caroline writhed beneath him, spurring him on, loving his touch, returning each caress with more of her own. She had never felt as alive or as complete as she did in his arms.

His hands sliding over her body electrified her, and she stroked his muscled form, eager to learn every inch of it. She might not remember the first time they made love, but she was building new memories she hoped would last a lifetime.

"Caroline!" Max gasped as she touched him before his lips took hers in a kiss that was the ultimate in oneness, a union of breath and spirit that filled Caroline with joy. When, together, they reached completion, she collapsed, exhausted yet content from their lovemaking. For the first time since her accident, she felt at peace, happy.

Max lay without moving for several minutes, unable to think. Their lovemaking had been even more stupendous than he'd remembered, something he hadn't believed could be possible. Eventually he shifted his weight, concerned with hurting Caroline.

"Max!"

"What is it, Caroline?" he asked, recognizing something unusual in her voice.

"Max, I hope you have some crackers."

He leaned back and stared at her. "Probably, but we haven't discussed eating crackers in bed. Don't you think you're moving a little fast here?"

"Very funny," Caroline replied faintly. "If you don't get me some crackers quickly, I'm going to throw up my breakfast in your bed. Which do you prefer?"

He leaped off the bed and raced to the kitchen without bothering to pull on his jeans.

"CAROLINE?"

She was leaning back against the booth at the restaurant where they'd eventually gone for lunch, replete, her eyes closed. "Hmm?"

"Caroline, what are you going to do?"

Her hazel eyes popped open and she lost her satisfied look. "What do you mean, Max?"

"What are you going to do about us?"

"I—I don't understand."

"I just made love to you. You made love to me. Doesn't that mean something?" He could feel the frustration rising in his voice, but he didn't know how to control it. The thought of Caroline leaving him, perhaps even seeing Adrian, drove him crazy.

"Of course it does. It was the most wonderful experience in my life."

"That you can remember," he reminded her, his voice heavy with sarcasm.

Her cheeks flushed and she stared at him, her chin raised. "Yes, that I can remember. Does that satisfy you?"

"No, it doesn't. We belong together. I don't want you to go back to your father's house. I want you to stay with me." He hadn't thought about the details. He just knew that she was his.

"Max, I can't do that."

She refused to meet his gaze and he felt he was fighting a losing battle.

"What do you mean?"

"I have to find out who the father of my baby is."

"Damn it, Caroline! I'm the father! I thought what we did was the proof you need," he growled.

Caroline looked around her as if she feared he'd be overheard. "Max, I loved what we—how we spent the past few hours, but that doesn't change the fact that you may not be the father."

"So what were we doing? Conducting a little test? Was that the real purpose of your visit? Comparison shopping? Are you going to try to remember with Adrian, too?"

He knew he shouldn't have said those things. He didn't even mean them. But he was frustrated . . . and afraid. He didn't want to lose her.

But it seemed he already had.

Since she'd left her car at his office, she couldn't leave without him, but she made her unhappiness obvious as she picked up her purse without a word and stood, waiting for him to join her.

Hastily paying the bill, he followed her from the restaurant. Once they were in his pickup, he tried to make amends.

"I'm sorry, sweetheart. What I said was out of line. I didn't mean to be hateful. I'm a jealous snake. Please forgive me."

She said nothing.

"Come on, Caroline, that was a pretty good apology. I haven't groveled like that in a long time."

"Pretty good? You think pretty good will do after saying such hateful things?" she exploded, and then looked away, folding her arms over her chest.

"I guess not," he muttered, watching her out of the corner of his eye.

After several minutes taut with tension, she murmured, "Do you really think I planned—"

"No, of course not. I'm sorry I even suggested such a thing." When she remained silent, he added, "Especially if you're not going to speak to me again." They'd reached his office and he parked the pickup and leaned forward to force her to look at him. "Are you?"

"I'm thinking about it," she said, obviously trying to hold back a grin. His mother always said he would tempt a saint. And, thank God, Caroline was no saint.

"How about if I take you out to dinner tonight, as an apology for my boorish behavior?"

"Since it's an apology, do I get to choose the restaurant?"

"Man, you drive a hard bargain. Okay, okay," he agreed, holding up his hand when she would've protested. "You can choose the restaurant, but please don't make me wear a tux."

"A tux?" she repeated, perking up at the suggestion.

He groaned. "I knew it!"

She leaned over and kissed him. "Never mind. I won't torture you that much. Why don't we go back to that Italian restaurant we visited the other night when Prescott joined us?"

"Are you sure? I'll spring for something fancier if you want."

His arm settled around her shoulders and he pulled her closer to him. Leaning into his chest, she whispered, "I don't need fancy when I'm with you."

His response consisted of several kisses so hot Caroline thought she'd be consumed by fire. A honking horn interrupted them, or they might have embarrassed themselves.

"I think I'd better go," she said shakily, moving away from his magnetic presence.

"Yeah, well, I'll pick you up at seven."

"Don't be late," she whispered with a grin, sliding from the truck.

"Not a chance."

He walked her to her car, gave her one more sizzling kiss, and then sent her on her way with a smile.

CAROLINE FORGOT any other errands she'd planned that day and headed for home. She was exhausted and intended to spend the rest of the afternoon taking a nap before she made herself pretty for Max.

Though she still didn't have proof that Max was the father of her baby, she just knew he was. After Max, there could be no one else. No other man could compare to him. He was the father of her baby. She was sure.

She called out to Mrs. Lamb as she entered the house, then started up the staircase, her smile still in place.

"Caroline?"

She paused, a sinking feeling in her stomach as she recognized Adrian's voice. Leaning over the stair railing, she saw him emerge from the sun room.

"Where have you been? I've been waiting for you."

Frowning, she moved back down several steps. "I don't remember making any plans with you, Adrian."

"No, I didn't mean we had plans. But I think you'll be happy with what I do have."

"What do you mean?"

"I brought proof." When she stared at him, saying nothing because she couldn't speak, he added, "I've brought proof that I'm the father of your baby. Now we can be married."

Chapter Eleven

"No!"

One blond brow rose as Adrian stared at her, giving him a quizzical look. "No?"

"You can't have proof," Caroline said, her voice shaking as much as her knees. Suddenly she plopped down on the stairs.

"Are you all right?" Adrian inquired in studied concern. "Perhaps you should lie down for a while. We must take care of our child...and you."

"No! No, I need to see the proof. I need to—"

"There's nothing you need to do. Your parents have already gotten the ball rolling. In days we'll be husband and wife."

Now wasn't the time to be weak. Caroline grasped the banister and pulled herself to her feet. As she came down the stairs, she demanded, "Where is your proof? I want to see it."

"Well, of course, darling. It's in the sun room. I left it on the coffee table."

"Caroline? Is that you?" Mrs. Lamb called, her voice preceding her through the door that led to the kitchen.

"Yes, Lambie. I'm here. Could you bring me some tea to the sun room?"

The housekeeper walked over and placed the back of her hand against Caroline's cheek. "Of course, but you look pale. Shouldn't you lie down?"

"Not right now. I have something to do." She managed to dredge up a smile before she turned to the sun room. Adrian was right behind her, his hand coming up to rest against the small of her back.

How could Adrian be the father of her child? She couldn't stand his touch. Max, on the other hand—that didn't bear thinking about.

When she reached the coffee table, she stared at the large manila envelope lying on it. She was afraid to look at the "proof." What if she couldn't refute it?

He reached around her and picked it up. "I had forgotten that we ordered the picture. It came in the mail at the office this morning. I went at once to your father. He agreed that it was conclusive evidence."

Adrian's smile reminded her of the cat that had swallowed the canary. It made her sick to her stomach. "What picture?"

"One night at dinner in Vegas. You know how those photographers come around and offer to take a picture of a momentous event." He put his arm around her shoulders. "I thought what was going on between us was fairly momentous."

"Tell me again what was going on between us," she suggested, moving away from him, putting off the moment of truth.

"I told you the other night. We were having an affair. But you wanted to keep everything a secret. Your father is the master of pressure, and you wanted to avoid that."

Even without her memory, she knew that her father always wanted his way and would do whatever to get it. That was what scared her. Adrian's story was so plausible.

Except for one thing.

She didn't want his touch.

Was it because she'd fallen for Max since she'd slept with Adrian? Could one extraordinary attraction wipe out the memory, the desire, for another's touch?

"How long had we been having an affair?"

"A couple of months. I'd been escorting you to some of the charity events, and one night we—well, we made love."

"Where?"

Both of his eyebrows shot up, as if the question surprised him.

"I can't remember!" she reminded him in frustration.

"My place, mostly. The first time, in the car."

"In the car? Like a couple of randy teenagers?" she demanded, horrified.

"Hey, there's nothing wrong with that. We were swayed by the moment." He leaned closer to say with a growl in his voice, "We're both passionate people."

She couldn't deny his assessment of her, not after her time spent with Max. But with Adrian? She stepped from his embrace to sit down in a chair. When Mrs. Lamb entered with the ice tea, she was grateful. She wasn't ready to look at the picture.

The cold drink revived her somewhat.

"Are you sure you shouldn't lie down?" Mrs. Lamb asked, hesitating before she left them alone.

"Maybe in a little while, Lambie. I'm fine."

Though she looked doubtful, Mrs. Lamb left the room. Adrian circled the coffee table and sat down on the end of the sofa nearest her.

"Don't you want to look at the picture? It's dated and everything."

"Dated?"

"Yeah. They do that on these professional photos," he explained, "kind of like they do on all the film these days." As he talked, he opened the envelope and slid out an eight-by-ten photograph.

Steeling herself for what she would see, Caroline held out her hand for the evidence. Adrian gave it to her and sat back against the cushions with a broad smile.

The photograph was of the two of them, her and Adrian. There could be no doubt of that, she realized, despair seeping into her heart. They were in a booth with the casino in the background, and she was snuggled against his shoulder while he had his arms crossed in front of him on the table. The date on the border of the photo read June 29.

"And you just received it today? Why did it take so long to send the picture?"

He shrugged his shoulders, undisturbed by her question. "Who knows? I figured we'd never see it. Some of these guys are fly-by-nighters. But you wanted the picture, so I paid."

He acted as if she should be grateful, she thought angrily. Instead, she'd like to tear the thing into small pieces. But that wouldn't erase the doubts the picture had put in her head. Or the despair.

"So, any more questions?" Adrian asked cheerfully.

"No, no questions." Not any that she could come up with at the moment. But something about the photo bothered her.

He leaned forward to take the picture, but she pulled back, pressing it to her chest. "No, no, I want to keep it."

"Now, come on, darling, let me have it. I'll get you a nice frame for it. We can show our child when he's older, explaining how the picture saved the day."

"I already have several frames. I'll take care of it."

"It's not the exact size. It'll need a special-sized frame," he explained, his smile not quite as relaxed.

"That's all right. I know a frame shop." The fact that he didn't want to leave the picture with her was the only encouragement she'd had the past ten minutes.

"Give me the name of the shop, and I'll drop the picture off on my way back to the office."

"Oh, no, it will be out of your way. I'll drop it off later." She watched with rising interest as frustration filled his face.

"You're going to be too busy, Caroline. After all, we have a wedding to get ready for."

"I don't think we have to be in a big rush. We have seven months before junior puts in an appearance."

The smile she was beginning to hate reappeared on his face. "Your father is much too impatient to wait any longer."

"I think it's my decision, not my father's."

Adrian laughed. "I guess you really did lose your memory if you think that. Your father is making all the arrangements right now. In three days, your wedding—our wedding will take place."

"Don't be ridiculous!" she exclaimed even as she believed what he was saying. How like her father! Without realizing it, she let the picture fall to her lap.

Instinctively, as she caught the rapid motion of Adrian's arm, she reached for the picture. It ripped in half, each of them holding a portion.

"Look at what you did!" Adrian exclaimed and reached for the other half.

Caroline pulled back, staring at the bottom half of the picture that she held in her hand. Suddenly, what had bothered her about the scene became obvious.

"I don't remember ever seeing this dress before."

"You lost your memory, remember?" His voice was heavy with sarcasm.

"But I've been through my closet. I didn't see a dress like this." In the photo she was wearing a tobacco brown linen coatdress with black trim on the collar.

"You bought it for the trip. That evening, the waiter spilled red wine on it. You ended up throwing it out."

"How convenient," she muttered, staring at the photo.

Adrian snatched it from her fingers, which she'd relaxed as she thought about what he'd said. "I'll have this mended. I know a good place. Then I'll buy a frame for it before I let you hold it again. That way it can't be destroyed."

He stood and walked over to the door. There he paused and said, "If I didn't know better, I'd think you weren't happy about our marriage. Fortunately, I haven't lost *my* memory."

His meaning didn't sink in until he'd left, closing the door behind him. Then she felt sick to her stomach. He was referring to their lovemaking. In a car, no less!

She couldn't imagine losing herself so much in a man that she'd— The sudden memory of those kisses Max had given her only a short time ago halted her protest. But that was with Max, not Adrian.

Could she respond to two men like that? At the same time? Of course, if Adrian was telling the truth, then today was the first time she'd slept with Max. And the last.

She buried her face in her hands.

Max.

Dear God, what was she going to tell him?

Afraid to put off calling him, in case she lost her nerve, she crossed the room to the telephone.

"Daniels Vacation Homes."

"Uh, Susan?"

"Yes?"

"This is Caroline Adkins. Is Max there?"

"No, Caroline, he's on a building site. Do you want me to beep him?"

She wasn't that brave. "No, just give him a message. I have to cancel our plans this evening."

"Okay. I bet he'll be disappointed. You sure did a lot to improve his mood today." Susan chuckled but Caroline didn't join in the laughter.

"Give him another message for me, please. Tell him—tell him Adrian has proof."

"Adrian has proof? Will he know what that means?" Suddenly Caroline felt like crying.

"Oh, yes, he'll know."

MAX PULLED INTO the parking lot outside his office with a grin a mile wide. Life was good! He'd just sold another home and he was having dinner with Caroline.

After a terrific lunch.

As he got out of the truck, he remembered the kisses they'd shared on the same spot before she drove home. She felt what happened between them, just as he did. He'd convince her the baby belonged to the two of them.

"Hi, Suze. Unless there's an urgent message, just hold them till tomorrow," he said as he sailed past his sister's desk and into his office. He wanted to have plenty of time to shower and shave for this evening.

Susan followed him to the door of his office. "The only important one was from Caroline."

"She called?" he whirled around. "What did she say? Am I supposed to call her?"

"She didn't say. She just said she had to cancel your plans."

"What?" he snapped, disappointment filling him. "Did she say why?"

"No, but she left another message. It didn't make sense to me, but maybe it will explain things to you. She said you'd understand."

"What?" he demanded impatiently. Sometimes Susan could drive him crazy with her details.

"She said 'Adrian has proof.'" Susan stared at him, but he couldn't respond. He'd turned to stone. "Do you know what that means?"

Anger welled up in him. "It means that bastard is lying!" he yelled. He brushed past his sister and headed for his truck. He was getting to the bottom of this "proof" at once.

Why would she believe Adrian? She hadn't believed *him,* in spite of the magic that happened every time they touched. What had Adrian given as proof? He'd probably bribed someone to say he saw them together. Or manufactured a receipt.

His mind played endlessly with the possibilities until he screeched to a stop at the closed gates. Mrs. Lamb opened the gates from the house without question and he was knocking at the door in no time.

"Come in, Mr. Daniels. Are you here to see Caroline?"

"Yes, I am. Is she in?"

"Yes. If you'll just wait here, I'll go see if she's asleep. She wasn't feeling too well earlier."

Max wanted to bound up the stairs ahead of Mrs. Lamb. He wanted to find Caroline himself. He wanted to see if she was feeling okay. He wanted to love her until she admitted the truth. That she was his. And he was hers.

And Adrian... and his proof... didn't exist.

He was pacing the entry hall when footsteps alerted him to Mrs. Lamb's return. He whirled to the stairs to find Caroline had accompanied the housekeeper.

She didn't look well.

"Are you all right?" he demanded, starting up the stairs.

"I'm fine. What are you doing here?"

He drew back, stunned by her question. "What am I doing here? What the hell do you think I'm doing here? After the message you left? You thought I'd just quietly slink away?"

"Mr. Daniels, I don't think—" Mrs. Lamb began, stepping in front of Caroline, as if to protect her.

"It's okay, Lambie," Caroline said softly. "He has reason to be upset. We'll just go into the sun room and talk."

"Shall I bring you something to drink?"

"No. We just need to—to talk."

Her admission that he had reason to be upset calmed Max, somewhat. That and her paleness. She looked ready to faint. He suddenly remembered that she'd only been out of the hospital with a concussion for about a week.

"Should you be out of bed?" he asked as he closed the door behind him.

She turned to face him, her gaze troubled. "I thought you wanted to talk to me."

With a groan, he closed the distance between them and wrapped his arms around her, feeling her softness the entire length of him. It drove him crazy.

She rested against him for a brief minute and then pulled away, going over to sit down in a stuffed chair.

He followed her, standing over her like a disapproving father. "Tell me."

She twisted her fingers together in her lap, staring at them as she talked. "He brought a picture of the two of us in Las Vegas. It was dated June 29. He said we'd been having an affair for a couple of months and went away together. I'd asked him to keep everything a secret because of my father."

He slid a finger beneath her chin and lifted her face. Staring into her hazel eyes, he asked, "Do you believe him?"

"I saw the picture, Max. It was me. I was there in Las Vegas. And if that's true, then I couldn't have been with you."

Ah. There was the crux of the matter. One of them was lying, he and Adrian, and Adrian had a photo. He had nothing. He hadn't thought of taking a picture of her because he'd wanted to believe he'd never lose her.

Leaning forward, he captured her lips with his. Her arms slid around his neck and he pulled her up against him as his tongue enticed hers and he kissed her down to her toes. When he finally pulled back, they both were breathing heavily. "Do you believe that? Do you feel that with Adrian?"

He almost thought he'd won when a glimmer of a smile filled her beautiful eyes. "You know I don't, Max. At least, I don't think I do. The man hasn't kissed me since I've been out of the hospital, but I can't imagine he would affect me like you do."

They looked at each other, Max sharing with her the astonishment he felt each time they touched. It had never been this way before, with any woman. Only Caroline.

"But that doesn't make it impossible that I might have slept with him before."

"Before you slept with me?"

Her teeth sank into her bottom lip. "Max, if the picture is the truth, then I hadn't slept with you until today."

"Then that picture is a damned lie!"

She reached out and smoothed his ferocious frown with her fingertips. "I want it to be, Max, but I don't see how—"

"I want to see it."

"I don't have it. It got ripped and Adrian took it to have it repaired."

Max noted that she was avoiding his gaze. He pulled her chin back around. "What aren't you telling me?"

"What do you mean?"

"There's something you're not telling me."

She hesitated and then said, "He was extremely reluctant to leave the picture with me." Before he could speak, she added, "But that's just an impression. It isn't proof."

He shoved himself away from the chair and stood. "And that's what you have to have, isn't it? Proof. My word means nothing. My touch that drives you crazy means nothing. You have to have proof!" He made the last word sound like something dirty. And it was. Because without proof, she wouldn't believe him.

"Max! I can't go on my instincts. There's more involved here. He may be the father of my child! I can't just tell my child someday that I don't know who his father is. That I wanted to be with you, so I ignored the truth."

He stared at her, unable to deny the pleading in her gaze. Reaching out, he caressed her cheek briefly. Even that small touch set his blood racing. He stepped back, breaking contact with her.

"Okay. I'm trying to understand. Just give me a little time, and I'll find my own proof somehow."

He thought he was being magnanimous, exhibiting incredible patience, when what he wanted to do was punch out Adrian. Or anyone else who got in his way.

One look at Caroline's face as she sank back down into the chair, and he knew she wasn't impressed.

"Max—" She broke off and looked away.

"Spit it out, Caroline. If you want me to get lost, just say so." His heart would break if she did.

She leaped to her feet and then almost passed out. He clutched her and held her against him, hoping and praying it wouldn't be for the last time.

"Well?"

"No, Max, I don't want you to get lost. The thought of not seeing you again—"

"Then what is it? What were you going to say?"

"I—I can't give you much time."

"Why? What are you saying?"

"I promised my father I'd marry the father of my baby as soon as we found proof."

"And you always keep your word," he muttered, rubbing her back, imprinting the feel of her in his heart.

She buried her face in his neck even as she nodded.

"How long do I have before you marry this jerk?"

He waited tensely for her to answer. When she said nothing, he wondered if she'd heard the question. Finally she lifted her head and stared up at him, tears in her eyes.

"Three days. The wedding is in three days."

Chapter Twelve

"Three days?" Max repeated, drawing back to stare at her. Anger rose within him. "How could you agree to such a thing?"

She stiffened, the tears disappearing. "I had no choice, Max. I've embarrassed my parents enough as it is."

"A little embarrassment is more important than the truth?"

"Max Daniels, the least you can do is understand! I can't help it if I can't remember. I don't know who's telling the truth. But Adrian came up with proof."

"Probably manufactured. How about a lie detector test? How about if Adrian and I take lie detector tests?"

"I doubt that Adrian would agree," Caroline said, her anger leaving her like a deflated balloon.

"I doubt it, too. Since he's won."

She said nothing, but the sadness in her eyes cut him to the quick.

"You're really going to go ahead with it?"

"I have no choice...unless something turns up that says he's lying."

His heart aching, Max stepped to her side. He had to touch her one more time. Pulling her to him, his lips took hers until both almost forgot he was saying goodbye. When he finally released her, he stepped back and said, "I'm not giving up, Caroline. That's my baby. I'll find a way to prove it to you."

Then he walked out of the house before he was tempted to carry her up the stairs to the nearest bed in a desperate attempt to convince her. Slamming himself into his truck, he burned rubber down the driveway.

Only as he headed back home did he calm down enough to think. She would marry that jerk Adrian unless someone found proof the man was lying.

Someone.

Who?

Him, of course. No one cared more than he did. It was up to him, Max Daniels, to find proof. Great relief filled him as he realized there must be something he could do.

His bubble burst when the next question occurred to him.

What?

What could he do?

He pulled to the side of the road. He had to figure out what to do and fast. There wasn't much time. He remembered reading an article in the paper recently about a private investigator. If he could remember the man's name, he'd call him. He pulled back onto the road and then off again when he reached the nearest gas station.

"Do you have a telephone directory, the yellow pages?" he asked the attendant.

The man readily handed over the thick book and Max thumbed through the listings.

"Damn! I'd better get help. I can't even find a telephone number," he muttered.

"What you lookin' for?" the attendant asked.

"A private investigator, but there aren't any listed."

"Sure there are. Look under 'detective.'"

Max briefly wondered why a gas station attendant would so readily know how to find such a listing. Then he dismissed that idea as he found the names of several detective agencies. He recognized the man's agency and wrote down the number on the back of an envelope he found in his pocket.

"Do you have a—" he began as he closed the book.

Divining his question, the man pointed to the telephone on the desk. "Use that one if it's local."

Much to Max's surprise, he received an immediate appointment with the detective in question. Getting directions, he rushed for his truck after thanking the gas station attendant.

The detective's office was modest but neat, nothing like the offices Hollywood always depicted. A sedate, middle-age woman greeted him and then announced his arrival to Don Knowles, the detective.

"Come in, Mr. Daniels. Have a seat and tell me what's on your mind."

After his eager rush to reach the man, Max found it difficult to explain his needs. The detective wasn't the problem. Like the receptionist, he was calm, quiet, middle-aged, redolent of respectability.

"It's difficult to explain."

"Just start at the beginning."

"A little over two months ago, I met a woman. Caroline Adkins." Max noted that the detective seemed to recognize the name. "We dated for two weeks. Then, one night at my house, we, uh, we got carried away."

Mr. Knowles didn't seem to need any amplification of that statement.

"She disappeared the next day."

"And you want me to find her?"

"No. I've found her. A week ago, I discovered she is the daughter of James Adkins."

"I thought so."

Max licked his lips. The story got a little more difficult to explain now. "Her name was given on the radio because she was in the hospital from an accident. She hit her head on the windshield and got amnesia." He shifted in his chair. "We all discovered at the same time that she is two months' pregnant."

The detective's eyebrows soared over his calm brown eyes.

"And three of us said, at the same time, that we were the father of her baby." Max paused, thinking about what he'd said. "I don't know if I said that correctly, but do you understand?"

"Yeah, I think I get the gist of it. You want me to find out who's the father?"

"No. I already know that. I'm the father. The other two both work for her father. They've got a lot at stake. Caroline and I eliminated one of them by his own admission. But the other one—he's come up with proof that he and Caroline were in Vegas the two weeks I *know* she was with me."

"What kind of proof?"

"A photo, taken by one of the professional photographers who roam the clubs. It's dated June 29."

Don Knowles leaned back in his chair. "Well, I think I've finally figured out what you want. You want me to prove the man is lying."

"Exactly. There are a couple of catches, however," Max added, wanting the man to understand the challenge he was giving him. "I don't have the photo, and I haven't seen it. And you only have three days."

CAROLINE FOUGHT HER WAY out of a deep sleep, something urging her to consciousness. Perhaps it was her stomach, but she had learned her lesson. She reached for the crackers and carbonated water Mrs. Lamb had begun leaving beside her bed every evening.

When she got her stomach under control, she turned her thoughts to the events of the previous day. After Max's departure, she'd had to deal with her parents' return and numerous questions.

Not about Adrian's revelation.

Her parents accepted the photograph as valid proof that she had been in Las Vegas with Adrian. And that he was the father of her baby.

She understood why her father wanted her to marry Adrian. And maybe it was guilt that kept her from refusing. Her father had counted on her to succeed him in the business. He'd brought her into the office right out of college, given her a lot of responsibility, shown absolute faith in her.

And two years ago, she'd walked out on him.

It had hurt to displease her father. She loved him. But she hadn't been happy working in the large corpora-

tion. The creative side of her was dying. She'd returned to school to get a degree in interior design.

Her father had never really forgiven her. Then he'd
come up with the plan to marry her to someone who
could take over the company. That's when he'd begun
promoting Adrian and Prescott. At least, she thought
so.

Between hating to disappoint her father a second
time, and fearing that Adrian might be the baby's father, she couldn't simply dismiss her promise. Her child
had the right to at least know his father, to bear his
name. Even if it was Adrian's.

So she understood why her father was pleased that
Adrian claimed to be the father. And her parents'
questions were about flowers, dresses, invitation list,
preference of colors, and other inane questions that
drove Caroline wild. How could she consider such ridiculous things when she was concerned with who the
groom would be?

Without conscious thought, she wandered over to her
closet. The dress wouldn't be there, Adrian had told her,
because she'd thrown it out. But something about that
dress bothered her.

She stared at the dual row of clothing, mulling over
the picture in her mind. It finally struck her. There
wasn't a single brown dress in her closet.

Not a single one.

Blue dominated the colors, a clear, bright blue. There
were some reds, a couple of hot pinks, lots of shades of
purple, an occasional green. Both white and black.

But no beiges, no browns, no yellows.

She turned to the phone and called down to Mrs. Lamb, asking for a breakfast tray. Slipping back into bed, with pillows propped behind her, Caroline waited.

When the housekeeper arrived, Caroline asked her to sit down and keep her company. "Mrs. Lamb, I've been looking at my wardrobe. I seem to like bright colors."

"Oh, my stars, yes, Caroline. You always pick bright colors. Chelsea likes pastels, but not you."

"Do I ever wear brown?"

"Only when you were in the Brownies," Mrs. Lamb said, chuckling. "I swear you quit because of the color of the uniform. I tried to persuade you to stay until you became a Girl Scout and could wear green, but you were stubborn, even then."

"So I never wear brown," Caroline muttered to herself.

"What is it, dear? Has something happened?"

"Do you know anything about photography, Mrs. Lamb?"

The lady stared at her. "Photography?"

"I know it doesn't seem connected to brown, but it is. Adrian showed me a picture yesterday of the two of us in Las Vegas, supposedly during those two weeks I was missing."

Realization dawned on Mrs. Lamb's face. "So that's why your parents are planning your wedding with him."

"Yes. But, Lambie, I was wearing a brown dress."

"Oh, my stars, that's impossible! You don't own a brown dress!"

"Adrian said I bought it for the trip and then threw it away after the waiter spilled wine on it." Mrs. Lamb's face reflected Caroline's own feelings. "It sounds rather convenient, doesn't it?"

"You think the picture is a fake?"

Caroline leaned back against her pillows and sighed. "I don't know. I don't even know if it's possible, because it was certainly my face."

"Of course it's possible. Why, those scandal sheets do things like that all the time."

"They do? Yes, I guess they do. I hadn't thought about it. I was so shocked—you're right. The picture is obviously a fake. And that's why he didn't want me to keep it."

"You don't have the picture?"

"No, he insisted on taking it with him." How she wished she'd been able to keep the picture.

"What are you going to do?"

Caroline set aside the tray and slid from the bed. "I'm going to find a way to prove Adrian is lying!"

After Mrs. Lamb took the tray and returned to the kitchen, Caroline picked up the phone and called her father's secretary. In minutes, she had the name of the security firm her father used.

She only had to give her name to be immediately put through to the head of the firm, Joe Perkins.

"Mr. Perkins, I have a personal job for you. Money is no object, but speed is."

When she finished the conversation, Caroline felt much better. After a quick shower, she searched her closet for an outfit that would allow for her gently swelling figure. It was too soon to be wearing maternity clothes, like Chelsea, but her own clothes were becoming a little uncomfortable.

Just as she was finishing buttoning her blouse, her mother knocked on the door.

"Oh, you're already up. Good. Chelsea can be ready at one for our shopping trip, so I suggested she come here at noon and dine with us. Before she arrives, we had better make some decisions. Otherwise Chelsea will want to offer her opinion."

Caroline noticed that her mother had a clipboard and appeared incredibly efficient, unlike her usual distant figure. Was this how she operated at the charities? No wonder she was so involved.

"Uh, Mother, I have to go out."

"Don't be ridiculous. We're planning a wedding. Besides, where would you go?"

"I have an appointment that's urgent. I'll try to be back by noon."

"But it's ten-thirty already. We haven't even chosen your colors." Amelia looked horrified at such a lapse.

"I love blue. See, that decision is already made." Caroline ran a brush through her hair, added a touch of powder to her nose and turned to leave the room.

"Neiman's is going to show us what they have in gowns already in stock this afternoon. Mrs. Mason is pulling your size."

Caroline thought of the tightness of her clothes. "Better ask her to pull a size larger, Mother. I'm not a size eight anymore."

"Perhaps you should diet."

With a laugh, Caroline kissed her mother's cheek. "I don't think so. Pregnant ladies shouldn't diet."

"Oh, I forgot."

"Then you're not embarrassed that I'm already expecting a child before my wedding?" Caroline asked the question lightly, but she waited anxiously for her mother's response.

"Of course not."

"Thanks, Mother. Oh, I need a recent picture of me. Do I have any?"

"Yes, of course, but I've already taken care of the picture to the paper." She added huffily, "They said they weren't sure they could use it with such late notice."

Caroline almost groaned aloud. That's all she needed, publicity. "No, not for the paper. Where is the picture?"

"In one of the photo albums downstairs."

"Could you find it for me? I don't know where the albums are."

Her mother gave her an exasperated sigh and turned to leave the room, Caroline on her heels. As she walked, she muttered, "Honestly, Caroline, you really should take more interest in things. I've showed you those albums a thousand times."

As she followed her mother downstairs, a thought struck Caroline. Maybe losing one's memory was hereditary.

JUST A FEW MINUTES before noon, Don Knowles's secretary buzzed him. "Don, Mr. Perkins is on line one."

Don grinned as he picked up the phone. He and Joe Perkins were longtime friends and sometimes helped each other out.

"Hi, Joe, how are you?"

"Fine, Don. But I need a little help, so I naturally thought of you."

"Yeah, just because I owe you one for that missing wife case." They kept a running tab of favors done, though they both knew it meant nothing if either needed help.

"Right. But this one is kind of bizarre... and there's a real time factor."

"I'll help if I can. I've got a case kind of like that, too. In fact, I was thinking about calling you."

"Oh?"

"Yeah, it involves an employee of Adkins Industries."

"So we trade. Me, first. This is the weirdest case I've ever heard of. This woman, my client, was in a car wreck and hit her head. She got amnesia—"

"And she's pregnant and doesn't know who the father is."

There was a tense silence until Joe said, his voice filled with suspicion, "How do you know that?"

"Because the guy who says he's the father of her baby just hired me."

"Max Daniels?"

"She told you about him?"

"Yeah. She wants him to be the father. And the other guy is one of James Adkins's right-hand guys."

"That would be Adrian Meadows."

"So, what's your take on Daniels?"

"I believed him. I've been doing some calling around, and he seems to be legit."

"How about we combine forces? Would it be a betrayal to your client? I think they both want the same thing."

"I agree. What do you have?"

"A picture of Miss Adkins, the name of the casino, the dates. I wanted to hire you for a quick trip to Vegas."

"I'll get an afternoon flight. I wasn't sure it would be worth it with three days and not knowing the casino. My client didn't have that information. I'll be over to pick up the info you have as soon as I make a reservation."

"Great. I'll gather everything I've got. While you're gone, I'll work on Adrian Meadows. We did a background check a couple of years ago. He came up clean, but at least we have some info on him."

"Right. Sounds good. The only problem we've got is time."

"Yeah. Time."

TIME.

It seemed to be racing by.

Max had done what he could, he decided, hiring Knowles. He'd liked the man. He only hoped he knew his business.

What else could he do?

Caroline was in the throes of planning a wedding. And he was trying to wreck her plans. Too bad all that work might go to waste. A sudden thought struck him.

It was bizarre.

Would Caroline agree?

He reached for the telephone.

"I'm sorry, Mr. Daniels," Mrs. Lamb replied to his request for Caroline. "She's out shopping with her mother. May I ask her to call you when she returns?"

"Yes, please. I'm at the office." He gave her his number. "Do you have any idea when she'll be back?"

"I would guess around four o'clock, but sometimes shopping takes longer than you think."

"All right, thanks. Ask her to call as soon as she gets back."

He piddled around the office most of the afternoon, as he had all morning, wrestling with the desire to call Don Knowles to see if he'd made any progress. With only three days, he shouldn't pester the man. Knowles would need all the time he could get.

Finally, when he'd almost given up on Caroline calling, he heard her voice on the other end of the telephone.

"How are you?"

"Tired. Mother and Chelsea took me shopping for—for a wedding dress."

"Did you find one?" He felt masochistic, asking, but he had to know.

"Yes. I'm sorry, Max, but I don't have any choice."

He thought she did, but he wasn't going to argue with her. "I'm trying to work things out."

"Me, too. I'm hoping something will happen, but I have to prepare for the wedding."

"Caroline... I have a bizarre idea."

"What?"

He heard the eagerness in her voice and it warmed his heart. She didn't want to marry Adrian any more than he wanted her to.

"If I manage to prove Adrian is lying before the wedding, then all your work will go for nothing."

She gave an abrupt chuckle. "I don't think I'll complain."

"Me, neither, but it seems a shame."

"Max, what's your point? Do you want me to marry Adrian?" She sounded confused and a little outraged. "Do you think this is what I want?"

"Of course not. But I just thought—it makes sense to me for us to apply for a marriage license, too, to be prepared, in case I find proof that I'm the father of the baby." As he intended to do, come hell or high water.

"You want me to apply for *two* marriage licenses?"

Max heard her incredulity and laughed. "I know it sounds weird, but then, the past week hasn't exactly been normal for either of us. And if your parents are anxious for you to marry, I want to be prepared."

"I'm not marrying just to please my parents."

"And I'm not asking you for that reason," he assured her impatiently. Why was she being so difficult?

"I'm marrying Adrian because I owe it to my baby."

He squeezed the receiver, wishing it was Adrian's neck he held in his hands. "Don't expect a thank-you card."

"What?"

"I don't think the kid is going to be grateful. Whether he's his dad or not! You're making a mistake, Caroline!"

"You think I should just wait until the baby is born, when Adrian has offered proof?"

"No, I think you should marry me, no matter what."

"You're asking me to marry you?"

"Well, of course, I am." He'd been planning to marry her since he first saw her. "I told you I'm the father of the baby. Of course, we're going to marry. Just as soon as I can prove Adrian is a liar," he finished, a touch of sarcasm in his voice. He wanted her to believe him, without his having to produce proof. But however he had to do it, he was going to claim her and his child.

"Okay, I'll go with you to get a license," she suddenly capitulated. A pleading note entered her voice as she added, "Just one thing, Max."

"Yeah, what's that?" he asked, willing to promise her anything.

"Could you hurry with that evidence?"

Chapter Thirteen

After Max told her he'd leave at once to pick her up for their trip to city hall, Caroline hung up the phone with a sigh.

Another marriage proposal.

As much as she wanted this one, she found an important ingredient missing. Max had said he was the father of her baby. He had said he wanted her. He'd proven that one, actually. But, like Adrian, he'd never said he loved her.

She wanted to believe he did.

Some vague sense of recognition filled her and she grasped for a memory she sensed was close. Feeling as if she were searching for something important in a dense fog, she struggled, determined not to lose that elusive feeling.

A rap on her door disrupted her concentration. Chelsea walked in.

"Caro, have you thought about the napkins? What do you want printed on them?"

"Surely there's not enough time for that," she protested with a sigh for her lost memory.

"With Daddy's money, there's always enough time. Now, what shall we put on the napkins?"

"My name and a question mark seems appropriate," Caroline muttered.

"Whatever do you mean? Aren't you marrying Adrian? This is not something to joke about, Caroline."

"You're telling me."

"Caroline!"

She heaved a colossal sigh. "All right, Chelsea. My choice is to print nothing on the napkins."

"I told you there was time. Now, do you want Caroline and Adrian, Adrian and Caroline, or the Meadowses."

"None of the above. If I have to go through with this wedding, I can do without one thousand reminders on paper napkins." She crossed her arms over her chest and glared at her sister.

"You don't *want* to marry Adrian?" Chelsea asked, horrified. "But he's the father of your baby!"

"So he says. I'm not sure."

"Caroline! This entire situation is so distasteful. I can't believe you have embroiled us in such a mess."

Caroline glared at her sister in disgust. "Oh, really! What about the time you cheated on your spelling test and got caught? *You* embarrassed all of us then. So don't be so high and mighty!"

"I can't believe you're still bringing that—Caroline, you remembered!"

Her knees suddenly shaky, Caroline sank down onto the edge of her bed. "I—I guess so."

"Has your memory returned?"

As if testing a sore muscle, Caroline probed the inner recesses of her mind, seeking the elusive memory she'd lost a week ago. Nothing.

"No." She wanted to cry, but even that release eluded her. "No, I don't remember."

"Well," Chelsea huffed, "it doesn't seem fair that you remember *my* embarrassing moments but not yours."

She gave her sister a weary smile. "No, it doesn't, does it?"

An unexpected touch of sympathy filled Chelsea's face. "Maybe you'd better lie down. You look exhausted."

"Thanks, Chelsea, but Max is coming to pick me up."

The silence that followed her response brought her head up. Chelsea was staring at her. "What?"

"Well, I don't mean to tell you your business, Caro, but you're marrying Adrian in two days. Don't you think it's a little inappropriate to be dating Max?"

Hysterical laughter bubbled up in Caroline. If Chelsea thought her going out with Max was inappropriate, what would she think of them applying for a marriage license? "It's not really a date, Chelsea. We just have something we have to do."

"Does Adrian know?"

"I don't think so."

Chelsea crossed her arms and looked down her nose at her sister. "I know you're older than me, but since I've been married for almost a year, I think I should give you some good advice."

"Please, don't."

"Caroline! It's very important that you and your husband be honest with each other. Don't start your marriage by lying to Adrian."

"Why not? He's lying to me," Caroline muttered, irritation getting the better of discretion.

"What do you mean?"

"Have you ever seen me wear brown?"

Chelsea looked at her with concern. "Caroline, I think you need to rest. I'll explain to Max that you're not well."

"You'll do no such thing! I'm not crazy, which is what you're really thinking. The picture Adrian showed me! I was wearing a brown dress in it."

"But you don't wear brown." The puzzlement in Chelsea's voice did Caroline's heart good.

"Exactly!" When Chelsea still seemed puzzled, she added, "I think he faked the picture. He was in Vegas with another woman, a woman who wears brown, and he had the picture altered!"

"But that would be lying."

Caroline shook her head, a weary smile on her face. "I know, little sister, I know."

"But why? I mean, you are attractive, Caroline, but there are other women who—I mean, you're pregnant! Why would he claim your baby if he's not— It makes no sense!"

"Yes, it does. Prescott admitted he'd lied because Daddy's going to select the second in command for his company very soon. Prescott doesn't think he'll have a chance if Adrian is Daddy's son-in-law."

Chelsea's mouth dropped open and she sank down onto the bed beside Caroline. "Oh, my, how despicable."

Caroline almost laughed. It wasn't often she and her sister were in agreement. At least she didn't think so.

"But why are you going to marry him if he's lying?" Chelsea finally asked.

"Because I can't show he's lying. He's offered proof, which is more than Max has done." She got up from the bed to pace across the room. "Besides, Daddy wants this marriage so badly. And if Adrian is the father of my baby, it doesn't seem fair to him or the baby to deny him his legal right just because I've fallen in love with Max."

"Can't you explain to Daddy? I know he's difficult but he loves you very much."

Caroline shrugged. "You can imagine Daddy's reaction if I told him I can't marry Adrian because I wore a brown dress."

"But you can't take sacred vows if you don't mean them!" Chelsea protested.

Caroline was coming to love her little sister in spite of her irritating ways. But sometimes her naiveté drove her crazy. "I'm going to do everything I can to be sure that doesn't happen."

"Good, because—"

The distant ring of the doorbell interrupted Chelsea. Caroline jumped up and then had to steady herself. Those abrupt moves reminded her of her pregnancy if nothing else did.

"Caroline, you must be more careful," Chelsea warned, supporting Caroline. "I always move slowly now."

Complacency was another of Chelsea's annoying traits.

"Thanks for the warning. I've got to powder my nose and comb my hair. That will be Max."

"I still don't think going with Max is right," Chelsea said, following her into the bathroom.

"Tough. I do, and that's what counts."

"But about those napkins?" Chelsea was back on that again. "Plain white, right?"

Caroline turned from the mirror and hugged Chelsea. "You get smarter every day, little sister."

"ARE YOU ALL RIGHT?" Max asked after several minutes of driving in silence.

Caroline continued to stare in front of her. "Yes. I was just thinking about something Chelsea said."

"She went shopping with you and your mother?"

"Yes."

"You were shopping all day? You must be exhausted."

"Not all day. But yes, I'm tired." She didn't mention how she'd spent her morning. What if the agency discovered nothing? Again she thought of Chelsea's words.

"Well, the license shouldn't take long, and then I'll take you to dinner and you can relax."

"Dinner? I'm not sure—"

"You owe me dinner, Caroline. You canceled last night, remember?" He reached over and took her hand, carrying it to his lips.

She shivered, reacting as she always did to his touch. Giving a halfhearted laugh, she said, "Chelsea said I shouldn't be dating you when I'm marrying Adrian."

"Maybe you won't be marrying Adrian. Maybe you'll be marrying me."

Maybe. Caroline sighed. Just one more question mark to add to her life. She only seemed to deal in question marks these days.

They had to rush to reach the office before it closed. When they entered, a gray-haired woman walked to the counter to greet them.

"My, you just made it. We close in fifteen minutes. How may I help you?"

Caroline was suddenly glad her father had taken care of the details of the marriage license with Adrian. She'd rather the woman not know this license would be Caroline's second in the same week.

"We need to get a marriage license."

The woman asked for their identification, gave them forms to fill out and then asked for the fee.

"Is that it?" Max asked.

"Yes, it is. You'll have your license just as soon as I enter your names into the computer."

"Computer?" Caroline asked nervously.

"Oh, my, yes, we're quite up-to-date. We have everything computerized," she explained as she typed their names into the computer. "Why, isn't that strange."

"What?" both Max and Caroline barked out.

"You're the second Caroline Marie Adkins to apply for a license this week." She hit several buttons and then turned to stare at Caroline. "You live at the same address. And have the same parents."

"I—I changed my mind."

"She hasn't made up her mind," Max said at the same time.

The woman stared at Max. "You knew about it? And it doesn't bother you that your fiancée has a license to marry another man?"

"It's a long story."

"But have you already married the man? Bigamy is against the law, you know."

"Of course, I know," Caroline said crossly. "I told you I changed my mind. There's nothing illegal about applying for more than one marriage license, is there?"

"Well, no, dear, I guess not."

The woman shot Max a sympathetic glance. Caroline looked the other way, unable to stand the embarrassment. The clerk took the opportunity to whisper to Max, "You really should reconsider before you pay for the license. There are lots of other women in the world. Especially for someone as handsome as you."

"Well, really!" Caroline protested, spinning around. "Does counseling come with the license, or does he have to pay extra?"

The clerk gave her a glacial stare. "It's free."

"Thanks," Max said, and Caroline was incensed to see he was hiding a grin.

"Is the license ready?" Caroline prompted.

"Yes, of course." The woman muttered under her breath to Max, "But you'd better think about the step you're taking. Marriage is a serious thing."

"I couldn't agree more," Max said with a smile, taking the license and putting it into his shirt pocket. "Thanks for your help."

Caroline opened her mouth to tell the woman what she thought of her assistance, and Max leaned down and kissed her.

"My fiancée says thank you, also," he assured the woman, and pulled Caroline from the office before she could contradict him.

"You were laughing!" she complained as the door closed behind them.

He chuckled again as he held her close to him, his hand rubbing her shoulder. "Now, sweetheart, you'll have to admit it was kind of humorous."

"No, I don't," she insisted stubbornly, even as she enjoyed his touch. She slipped her arm around his waist and leaned against his chest as they continued to walk. "Well, maybe I do. I think I'm so tired I've lost my sense of humor."

He pulled them to a stop. "Would you rather go home and go to bed? I'll understand if you do."

"No. I want to have dinner with you, but I'd like to go home and change. I meant to do so before you got there, but Chelsea came up to talk to me and I forgot."

"Sure. We'll go back to your house and you can change."

Once they were in his truck and headed back on the freeway, Caroline said, "You know, that's another thing."

"Am I supposed to know what you're talking about?" he asked, squeezing her hand as he held it against his thigh.

"Sorry, I was thinking aloud. You always touch me."

"You're complaining?" he asked, startled.

"No! No, I love it, just as I love touching you. But Adrian doesn't touch me."

"He'd better not!"

His jealousy pleased her, but it wasn't her point. "No, Max, think about it. If we were sleeping together on a regular basis, as Adrian says we were, wouldn't he be used to touching me?"

He leered at her. "It's hard to sleep together and not touch."

She chuckled, as he'd intended, and leaned her head on his shoulder. "I mean when we're not in bed. We're touching. That's the first thing you do when we meet. You reach for me, whether it's my hand, my mouth, my shoulders, you touch me."

"You're pretty hard to resist."

"Adrian doesn't seem to have any trouble."

"You want him to touch you?" Max sounded jealous.

"Don't be silly. I'm just trying to think rationally about what's happening here."

"I agree with you, Caroline, but I don't think that line of reasoning is going to impress your father... or anyone else. And if you tell Adrian that, he'll just start touching you, to prove you wrong."

"I'll keep it to myself, then."

"Good girl," Max agreed, dropping her hand to put his arm around her shoulders and cuddle her close against him.

They pulled into the driveway and paused at the closed gate, Max pushing the button. While they waited for a response, he kissed her, a kiss that roused the desire simmering just below the surface every time they were close to each other. His hand was caressing her breast as the intercom came on.

"Yes?"

Max reluctantly pulled back, his gaze still on Caroline, as he answered Mrs. Lamb. After the gate swung open, he drove up to the house.

Just as he stopped the truck, Caroline said, "Oh, Max, I think I should tell you that there's a camera attached to the intercom system. Mrs. Lamb saw everything we did."

Like a schoolboy caught looking at dirty pictures, he flushed bright red up to his hairline.

"And that will teach you to laugh when *I'm* in an embarrassing situation," she teased before slipping from the truck.

With a growl, Max came racing around the truck and she scampered ahead of him into the house, laughing at his antics.

Until she almost bumped into Adrian.

And her father.

"Oh! Hi."

"Where have you been?" her father demanded.

Though he was speaking to her, James's stare was directed at Max.

"I had an errand to run."

"And you couldn't do it alone?" James demanded.

The seriousness of the situation eluded Caroline, especially when she applied his question to the past hour. "No, I don't think so."

"I find it inappropriate for my fiancée to be running around town with another man," Adrian said stiffly.

Caroline stared at the man she was supposed to marry in two days and remembered Chelsea's words. "Then perhaps I shouldn't marry you, Adrian."

Both her father and Adrian stared at her as if she'd just announced the outbreak of World War III. Max's hand came to her shoulder.

"Don't be ridiculous!" her father sputtered. "You promised to marry the father of the baby!"

"That's right," Adrian chimed in. "And I presented proof. That's more than *he* did."

"Adrian, I know I promised to marry the father of my baby. But I don't love you. I think it would be wrong for us to marry. I'd like you to release me from my promise." She wasn't sure when she'd made the decision, but Caroline felt she was making the right one.

Adrian's face took on a hurt expression that even convinced Caroline, making her uneasy. "I realize you don't care for me anymore, Caroline, but I think you owe me the right to make my child legitimate, to be its legal father. If, after it's born, you don't feel you can live with me, then we'll discuss a divorce. But at least give me the right to protect my child."

In spite of herself, his speech touched her. And made her angry. Even though she thought he was lying, he'd certainly made her feel like a despicable person, a fickle female, toying with his heart.

Before she could answer, Max said, "You aren't the father of her baby, Meadows, and you know it."

James answered before Adrian could. "I've seen his proof. Do you have any? Have you shown us anything to convince us that you're telling the truth and not just attempting to feather your nest with my fortune?''

"Daddy!" Caroline protested even as a sharp pain hit her between the eyes.

"I'm sorry, Caroline, but you have to be careful. I've warned you about men using you to get to me. And yet you still believe him."

"I don't care anything about you or your fortune!" Max roared. "All I care about is Caroline!"

"Easy to say, but like James said, I don't see any proof," Adrian taunted, triumph in his voice.

Chapter Fourteen

"What do you have?" Joe Perkins asked, gripping the telephone receiver tightly.

"Nothing so far. You?" Don Knowles asked in return.

"Nothing. This man covers his tracks well. I think there's another woman, but I can't find any proof of it."

"Several people have recognized the picture of Meadows you gave me. He was a tightwad tipper. But not the picture of Miss Adkins. They remember he was with a woman, but they're sure it wasn't her."

"Have you tried to find the photographer?"

"Yeah. There must be a million of them. I've looked at so many photos, I'm going crazy. I've got three more photographers to check out. Two of them are on vacation. The third one has disappeared."

"The wedding's tomorrow."

"Yeah, I know."

CAROLINE SLEPT LATE the next morning. The day before had exhausted her. And also frustrated her.

She was sure Adrian was lying, but his request to be the legal father of his own child, as he said, put her in a difficult position. And easily convinced her father her behavior was outrageous.

If she simply refused to marry Adrian, she would be alienated from her father. She didn't want that. Her family might not be like most families, but she loved them.

She reached for her crackers and nibbled slowly. How long before she got past morning sickness? Chelsea was six weeks ahead of her and she had no trouble with it.

Six weeks? Surely she wouldn't have to wait so long.

By then she supposed her fate would be sealed. All the mental debating would be over. And if she could find a way to avoid marrying Adrian, she'd just have to find a way to bring her father around.

"Too bad he's such a hardhead," she muttered. Though she really couldn't complain since she shared that particular trait.

And in spite of his great disappointment when she'd left his company, he'd supported her decision. Which made it all the more difficult to consider hurting him again. Which also explained why she was still living at home instead of having her own place, as she wanted.

With a sigh, she sank back into the pillow, covering her eyes. Too many decisions. Too many people to please. Too much she couldn't remember.

The phone rang. She checked her watch. Ten o'clock. "Hello?"

"Good morning, Caroline."

Max's baritone warmed her to her toes.

"Mmm, good morning," she replied, snuggling into her pillow, wishing it was Max's shoulder.

"Are you feeling okay after yesterday?"

"Yes. I'm just not moving very fast."

"I guess Adrian hasn't confessed all?"

At dinner last night, they had discussed such a possibility, but they'd both admitted it wasn't likely.

"No. And Daddy is firmly entrenched on his side."

"Yeah. I gathered that. I think my first clue was the glares he kept shooting my way."

"It's not you personally, Max. He just wants me to marry Adrian. He probably already has the honeymoon planned."

"Without consulting you?"

"Given the choice, my father would plan my entire life without consulting me. He always thinks he knows best." Even as she finished talking, a sudden thought struck her. "Max! What about after the wedding?"

"That depends on whose wedding."

"No, Max, think! If we were getting married tomorrow, wouldn't you have made plans for afterward? Where we would live, where we would go?"

"We *are* getting married tomorrow, and I was hoping you'd want to live in my house. And I know what room we'll be spending all our time in."

Caroline shivered under the covers as she thought about the time already spent in Max's beautiful bedroom. "Oh, Max, I would love it, but that's not the point."

He chuckled. "It never seems to be with you."

"Max! Stop teasing. Don't you see? Adrian hasn't made any plans for after the wedding. At least, I don't

think he has." Somehow she thought she was on to
something here. "I think I should go to Adrian's
apartment. Maybe I'll find something there that will
give us proof."

"You're not going to that man's apartment alone!"

"Well, it wouldn't be appropriate to take *you*."

"Look, sweetheart, I wasn't going to tell you because I didn't want to get your hopes up, but I hired a
private investigator."

"You did?"

"Yeah. So let him do the investigation, okay?"

"I hired one, too." She waited for his response, but
he remained silent. "Max? Are you there?"

"Yeah. I'm just surprised."

"Why? Did you think I wanted to marry Adrian?"

"No, but—have they found anything?"

"No. At least, they haven't called me. Yours?"

"No. I called this morning and his secretary said he
was in Vegas, working on it."

"I'll call mine."

"Call me right back," Max insisted.

"Okay."

Two minutes later, she called Max. "He said they
think there's another woman, but he has no proof. He
sent a woman to the office this morning, hoping to get
something out of his secretary, but she wouldn't tell her
anything."

"Damn."

His forlorn tones made her want to put her arms
around him. That and her desire to make love with him
again. Were pregnant women supposed to think about

such things? She'd better get her mind on important matters. "That's why I need to go to his apartment."

"Promise me you won't go alone."

Caroline promised and then hung up the phone reluctantly. She hated to break contact with Max. As long as she was with him or talking to him, she believed that they would somehow find a way to be together. And she desperately needed to believe.

Her body craved Max's. But even more importantly, her heart wanted him by her side. Forever and ever. She wanted to know that whatever she faced, Max would be by her side, sharing her life.

At least she'd found something she could do, and she felt a sudden burst of energy. She called her sister, hoping to persuade her to accompany her.

"Well, of course, you should see where you're going to live. Do you want to start moving your things?"

"No, Chelsea. I just want to see his apartment. Will you come with me?"

"I suppose so," Chelsea agreed with a sigh. "But I must say, your wedding is consuming all my time."

"Sorry," Caroline apologized meekly, but she suspected Chelsea would've expected so much more had it been her wedding.

An hour later, with Chelsea driving, they arrived at the address her father's secretary had given them. Caroline was determined to see the apartment without telling Adrian.

The security guard in the lobby of the high-rise apartment building smiled at them as they approached.

"Good morning, ladies. May I help you?"

"Yes, you can," Caroline assured him, hoping her confidence would sway him. "I need you to let me in to my fiancé's apartment." She giggled and fluttered her lashes. "He forgot to give me the key, and we're getting married tomorrow."

The man's smile took on a paternal air. "Now, just who would that fiancé be?"

"Adrian Meadows."

The smile disappeared.

"Mr. Meadows didn't say anything about getting married. And I've never seen either one of you with him before."

Chelsea appeared affronted by his words. "Certainly not. I'm a married woman."

"You haven't ever seen me before?" Caroline asked. "Not even in the evenings?"

"I don't work the late shift."

"Oh. That would explain it." She'd hoped she'd maybe found more proof, since Adrian said they made love in his apartment most of the time. Maybe she could find the night man. "But it's all right. I'm his fiancée."

"I'll have to call Mr. Meadows for his approval."

"Oh, surely that's not necessary. After all, after tomorrow, I'll be living here, too." She hoped she wasn't, but so far she wasn't making much progress.

The man ignored her and picked up the phone.

"I think this man is rude," Chelsea complained in a whisper. "You should complain to Adrian."

"What's your name?" the security guard asked.

"Caroline Adkins."

He repeated the name to whomever he was talking.
"Yes, ma'am. Just a minute." He held the phone out to
Caroline. "His secretary wants to talk to you."

"Hello?"

"Miss Adkins, this is Mary Lambert. Mr. Meadows
is out of the office at the moment. You needed to see his
apartment?"

"Why, yes. Since we're being married tomorrow—"
The sound of the phone hitting the floor stopped Caroline. "Hello?"

"I'm sorry, I dropped the phone. You're being married tomorrow, you were saying?"

"Yes, Adrian and I are being married tomorrow. I
thought I should see where I would be living."

"I expect Mr. Meadows to return in an hour. I'll have
him call you when he comes in." She sounded as if she
was about to hang up the phone.

"Wait! Can't you just tell the guard to let me in? I
don't want to have to make another trip over here."

"I'm afraid I can't do that, Miss Adkins. I'll have
Mr. Meadows call."

Caroline was left holding the receiver, the dial tone in
her ear. She looked at the guard, watching her intently,
wondering if she could fake her way past him, but it
didn't look promising. Finally she handed the phone
back to him. "He's out of the office."

"Maybe he's with Daddy," Chelsea offered.

"Of course. Why didn't I think of that? May I borrow your phone again?"

The guard reluctantly handed over the phone and
Caroline dialed her father's office.

"Daddy? Is Adrian with you?"

"Yes, he's here, but we're in the middle of a meeting. What do you need?"

"I want to see his apartment, to see where we'll be living, but the guard won't let me in." She hoped her voice conveyed some enthusiasm for the prospect of living with Adrian.

"Oh. Of course. Adrian, you need to give the guard at your condo permission to let Caroline in. She wants to see your place, though I guess she's seen it a few times, hasn't she?" he added with a chuckle.

Caroline wished she'd been able to see Adrian's face. Finding him with her father was so much better than him being in his office, alone. She heard a strangled protest.

"Why not?" her father asked, plainly puzzled. There was a mumbled response that Caroline couldn't understand.

"Adrian says the place isn't clean. He'll show it to you this evening."

"But aren't we having the rehearsal this evening? After all, the wedding is tomorrow night," Caroline insisted.

"No, your mother called and they've scheduled the rehearsal tomorrow at three."

"The day of the wedding?"

"Yes, Caroline, and I really have to get back to the meeting. Be a good girl, and Adrian will take you to his place this evening."

She hung up the phone. "I don't want to see it this evening!" she protested bitterly to her father, who could no longer hear her. Chelsea and the guard stared at her.

"Come on, Chelsea, let's go."

The guard said nothing as they walked away.

"What did Daddy say?"

"He said Adrian would show me the apartment this evening. After he cleans it. Can you see Adrian pushing a vacuum cleaner?" Just the thought cheered her, but she also knew that she'd lost the opportunity to surprise him. If she had to look at the apartment tonight, there wouldn't be a single shred of evidence.

"I'm not surprised you're irritated," Chelsea agreed. "Why, when Roddy and I were getting married, we made all our decisions together, picked out the house and furnished it before the wedding."

"Yes, but you had more than three days."

"Well, of course. It takes months to plan a wedding." Chelsea apparently realized she might have caused her sister concern. "I'm sure your wedding will be nice, too, Caro, but—but it would've been better if you'd had more time."

"Yes."

More time to catch Adrian in his lies.

More time to recover from her accident.

More time to remember.

Max waited impatiently for Caroline to call. She'd promised to do so as soon as she came back from Adrian's apartment.

There must be something he could do. He felt so helpless, letting others search for clues.

"Max?" Susan said from the door of his office. "While you were on the phone, a couple called to set up an appointment to see the house on Crider Lane. I made it for tomorrow evening at seven."

"Tomorrow? No, I can't make it."

"But Max, they sounded really enthusiastic. They've looked at it already. I think they'll buy it."

"See if Jim or someone can be there. I'll be busy tomorrow night."

"I didn't know you had anything planned. What are you going to do?"

Too bad she was his sister. Had Susan been a real secretary, he could have told her to mind her own business.

"Sorry, I should've let you know."

"You're going out with Caroline, aren't you? I don't know why you're keeping it a secret. I've already met her." Before he could say anything, she added, "First thing you know, the two of you will be looking at rings."

He stared at her. Rings. He'd never thought of that. Without another word, he got up and headed for his truck.

"Max? What did I say? Where are you going?"

"I'll be out of the office the rest of the day. And tomorrow, too."

He slammed the door of his truck and gunned the motor. Rings. He certainly was not going to use a ring purchased by Adrian Meadows. If he got the chance to marry Caroline tomorrow, she would wear *his* ring, not Adrian's.

Though his first impulse was to go to a jewelry store and buy a ring at once, almost as a talisman to prove he had a chance of marrying her tomorrow, he reluctantly decided he should consult Caroline first. He would go to her house and wait for her to return.

Mrs. Lamb opened the gate and met him at the front door.

"Caroline hasn't returned?"

"No, she hasn't. Would you care to wait?"

"Yes, thank you."

She stood back to let him in. "I'm afraid we're a little topsy-turvy with all the activities for the wedding."

"Who was it, Mrs. Lamb?" Amelia asked, coming into the foyer. "Oh, it's you, Mr. Daniels."

"Yes, ma'am. I'd like to wait for Caroline's return if you don't mind."

"Of course not. In fact, you can make yourself useful. We need another pair of hands. You don't mind, do you?"

Good manners insisted he agree, but he wondered what he was getting himself into.

"Good. Come with me. I've ordered some things for Caroline and they've just arrived. You can help me open boxes to see if the order is complete. The women I hired this morning have been on the phone calling to invite guests, so they're too busy. And Mrs. Lamb is constantly having to open the door. Presents have already started arriving."

Somehow, Caroline's mother didn't feel his opening boxes of lingerie for Caroline, the woman he loved, that she would wear for another man, was inappropriate. He certainly found it interesting as he held up scraps of lace. His imagination worked overtime picturing Caroline in those garments.

And made him more determined than ever that *he* would be the husband, not Adrian.

"Well, the order is complete. And I don't think I've forgotten anything. Where is Caroline? She needs to start opening the gifts. We have to record them or she'll never get the thank-you notes right."

During their inventory of the lingerie wardrobe, Mrs. Lamb had brought in numerous deliveries of gifts. Max was astounded at how complicated things could become in three days.

"You'll just have to start opening the gifts, Max, and I'll write down who they're from. Let me get pencil and paper."

"Yes, ma'am."

"Oh, call me Amelia. You've been very helpful."

Max watched her leave the room and then stared around him at the neatly folded stacks of lace and satin. Caroline wouldn't need to buy lingerie for several years. Which was a good thing when he saw the price tags.

He picked up a teddy, one that had particularly intrigued him, in bridal white. Yeah, Caroline would look terrific in that.

"Max! What are you doing?"

The woman in his head had suddenly appeared in the doorway. He quickly dropped the teddy.

"Uh, inventorying your new lingerie." The stunned look on her face amused him. "It was your mother's idea. Next, we're going to open your wedding gifts."

"You can't be serious," she protested.

"That would be highly inappropriate," Chelsea chimed in, looking over her sister's shoulder.

Amelia appeared behind them. "Oh, hello, I'm glad you're back. There's so much to do. Caroline," she continued as she pushed past her daughters, "I bought you new lingerie as a wedding gift. Max has been so helpful. I believe they sent everything I ordered. Isn't that right, Max?''

''Yes, Amelia, every item.'' He grinned at Caroline.

''Mother, you shouldn't have asked Max to help with my lingerie.''

Amelia turned to her in surprise. ''Well, I had to have some help, Caroline. You and Chelsea certainly weren't available. Now, there's quite a lot more to do. We must begin opening the gifts and recording them so you can start on the thank-you notes. I'm sure Max will help. You've been such a dear, Max.''

''Thank you again, Amelia, but I'm afraid I'll have to borrow Caroline for a little while.'' He'd like to do more than borrow her. The sexy lingerie gave him all kinds of ideas about what he'd like to do with Caroline.

The approving smile Amelia had been sending his way disappeared. ''What? Don't be ridiculous. Caroline can't leave. She has too much to do.''

''What is it, Max?'' Caroline asked, crossing the room to his side.

He liked the concern in her voice, her instant attention. He took her hand in his and whispered, ''We need to buy rings for the wedding tomorrow.''

Staring up at him, she blinked several times, as if having difficulty understanding. ''But, Max—''

''What are you two whispering about?'' Amelia demanded.

''Umm, Max and I need to talk—alone. We'll be right back,'' Caroline promised, pulling him toward the door.

"I certainly hope so. I have several things for Max to do. He's such a helpful man."

"Thanks for being so helpful!" Caroline exclaimed in exasperation, raising her eyebrows at him as soon as they were in the foyer. He pulled her into his arms in spite of her protests.

"You wanted me to refuse to help your mother? I don't want to start off my marriage with my mother-in-law unhappy with me."

"Max, you talk as if we're—as if it's our wedding." Caroline looked away from him. "I may have to marry Adrian."

He took her chin in his fingers and turned her back to look at him. "No. You're going to marry me. Those detectives will find something. You've got to believe that, sweetheart." His lips briefly touched hers. He couldn't risk losing control at the moment. But, oh, how he wanted to.

"I want to believe, Max. But we're almost out of time."

"We'll make it. And when we do, I'm not about to use a ring purchased by Adrian. So, we've got to go pick out a ring now, so they'll have time to size it."

She stared up at him, unsure, and he hoped she wouldn't refuse his request. Ever since the idea of a ring occurred to him, it had been growing stronger in his mind. He wanted a ring, his ring, that would show that Caroline belonged to him. He breathed a sigh of relief when a grin slowly appeared on her face.

"Two grooms, two licenses, why not two rings? And one for you, too?" she asked. When he nodded, she added, "After all, I seem to be doing everything in pairs."

"I guess I should've told you twins run in our family," he said.

"Don't joke, Max," she protested, her grin still in place.

"Uh, Caroline, I'm not joking." And he wasn't. Hoping to distract her from his latest revelation, he pulled her against him and tasted her lips again. He couldn't stand to hold her and not kiss her. Especially after picturing her in that teddy.

"Caroline? What—" Amelia's voice intruded on the kiss, and Max slowly released Caroline.

"Well, really, Max, you've been very helpful, but I don't think that kind of behavior is appropriate," Amelia protested. "Why, it's almost as if you were the groom instead of Adrian."

His gaze still trained on Caroline, he said, "We have to keep our options open, Amelia. There could be a last-minute change."

"Oh. Does Adrian know?" Amelia asked, a confused look on her face.

Chapter Fifteen

"Does Adrian know what?" James Adkins asked as he entered the house.

Caroline turned to face her father, but she remained in Max's arms. It was her mother, however, who answered her husband's question.

"That there may be a change of grooms. I certainly was surprised, and I would imagine he is, too." She paused, studying Max. "But I must admit, Max, you have definitely been more congenial than Adrian ever is."

"What are you talking about?" James demanded in his normal roar. "Adrian is the groom. He had proof!"

"Daddy, I don't believe his proof," Caroline said, trying to keep her voice calm.

"Why not?" James set his briefcase down on the floor and put his hands on his hips. "Give me a reason."

"I was wearing a brown dress!" she replied in exasperation.

"What? What does your dress have to do with anything?"

"I didn't know you ever wore brown, dear," Amelia commented, looking at Caroline in continued confusion.

"I agree," Chelsea said as she came into the foyer.

"Caroline, don't tell me you're turning into your mother? You've always been the sensible one," James moaned, slapping his forehead with his hand.

Chelsea was the only female to protest his criticism. Her wail about her father not loving her was background to the anger Caroline felt as she said, "I am sensible, but no more than Mother and Chelsea. They both realize something is wrong. Why don't you?"

"The only thing wrong is you won't do what you're supposed to."

"According to whom?" Caroline asked, moving closer to her father, challenging him.

"According to me! I'm your father! And you promised!"

"So, you don't care about my happiness?"

"I didn't say that!" James protested.

"I made you a promise, and I'm going to keep it, Daddy. Even though I know I didn't keep the promise I made you about work, I will keep this promise. But I want a promise from you." Caroline watched her father squirm. He loved tying others down, but he hated it himself.

"What promise?"

"If I find proof that Adrian lied, then you must be happy with my decision, whatever it is." She held her breath. Even if she didn't marry Adrian, that didn't mean her father would accept Max. Unless he made this promise. He kept his promises.

James met Caroline's gaze. "Very well. I promise. But it has to be good proof. I don't think Adrian would lie. He's an honorable man."

"Is he?" Caroline asked. "What was his reaction when I wanted to see his apartment?"

"He wants to make sure it's tidy for you. There's nothing wrong with that. We men aren't as neat as women." James's voice sounded sure, but Caroline noticed that his gaze shifted from hers.

"*I* think he wants to get rid of evidence," she said with determination.

"Evidence? You're beginning to make this whole thing sound like an episode of 'Perry Mason.'" He stared at each of them before bringing his gaze back to Caroline. "Why? Just because of a brown dress? You put her up to this, didn't you?" James asked, swinging his gaze to Max.

"Not the brown dress bit," Max said. "I'm afraid I wouldn't have noticed anything like that. Besides, I didn't see the picture. Did you?"

"Of course I did. In spite of what she said, I care about Caroline's happiness."

His gruffness touched Caroline and she hugged him briefly. "I know you do, Daddy. But there's more."

"More what?"

"More evidence," Caroline assured him, taking his hand and pulling him toward the sun room.

"Adrian has more proof?"

"No, Daddy. *I* do."

Everyone followed them.

"Then why haven't you told anyone?" Chelsea asked.

"Yes," James agreed, "why haven't you produced this evidence? Where is it? I want to see it."

Caroline regretted her impulsive words. "Well, I can't exactly *show* it to you." She felt better when Max moved to her side, his arm going around her waist.

"Just as I thought. You don't have any proof," James said triumphantly.

"What about the fact that Adrian never touches me?"

"I've seen him touch you. He took your hand the other evening."

"That's not—"

"Besides," James continued, ignoring her response, "it's probably because this—this stranger is always pawing you."

Max stepped away from her, his arm falling to his side, as if guilty of some great sin.

Caroline swung around to glare at him. "Are you going to let him intimidate you?"

"No," Max answered in measured tones, as if he resented her question. "But I am a guest in his house and you are his daughter." He raked his hand through his dark hair. "Besides, I told you you couldn't convince your father with that."

"Aha! So, it's a conspiracy!" James exclaimed.

"Don't be ridiculous!" Caroline shouted, swinging back to face her father. "Men! Mother and Chelsea understand. Why can't the two of you?"

"Because men have to have facts," Amelia said calmly. "I learned that a long time ago."

"Some women do, too," Max murmured, reminding Caroline of how often she'd said she had to have proof.

"Daddy, I hired the Perkins Security Firm to find out if Adrian is telling the truth," Caroline said. "I will keep my word if he really is the father of my child, but I will not be trapped by some money-hungry liar!"

"You what? You can't hire them! They work for me!"

"Afraid they'll discover the truth?"

"No! There's nothing to discover!"

"Then you have nothing to worry about." She turned to Max. "Come on, Max. Let's go."

"Go where?" James demanded, catching her arm.

"Out!" She pulled her arm from his grasp, slid her hand through Max's arm and headed for the door.

"Will you be home for dinner?" Amelia asked, as if the past fifteen minutes had never occurred.

"No, I'll take her out to dinner," Max said.

"But Adrian is coming over to take you to see his apartment," James protested.

"I don't want to see it now. I wanted to see it this morning." She didn't care if she did sound petulant. She couldn't bear the thought of an entire evening in Adrian's company.

"What difference does it make whether it's morning or evening, Caroline? You're being ridiculous."

She ignored him and pulled Max through the door.

"What am I going to tell Adrian?" James asked, coming after them.

Swinging around, she glared at her father. "Tell him he'd better be sure he's telling the truth. If he's lying, he's going to be sorry."

After they reached Max's truck and drove away, he asked, "Have you calmed down yet?" He reached over and took her hand.

"Probably not. Did I scare you?"

"Nope. I just wondered if you and your father have a shouting match every time you disagree."

"How would I know?" she demanded, glaring at the man she loved.

"Hey, don't start on me. I'm the innocent party, here."

"Yeah, sure. That's why I throw up every morning."

He grinned. "I'll take credit for that, sweetheart, but not the mess we're all in. If you hadn't run away, we'd be planning our nursery now."

She smiled back at him, but he'd touched on the one point in his version of her missing two weeks that always bothered her. "You have no idea why I left?"

His smile disappeared. "No. I racked my brain for hours, days, trying to figure it out. I alternately cursed you and called for you." He carried her hand to his lips. "I told myself, after a while, that I was glad you were gone. But the minute I knew where you were, I came running."

Whatever her reason for leaving, Caroline was happy he'd come. Even without her memory, she knew that Max Daniels was her soul mate, the one man in the world who could stir her senses, make her world complete. Leaning her head against his shoulder, she whispered, "I'm glad."

THE RING SELECTION didn't take long. They discovered they had the same tastes in rings. As soon as Caroline accepted Max's ability to buy the expensive ring she'd fallen in love with, their decision was made. Max chose a simple gold band, pleasing Caroline. She'd never liked diamonds on a man.

They enjoyed a quiet meal at a Mexican restaurant, another taste they discovered they shared. When the bill came, Max slipped out his charge card and laid it on the tray with the bill.

"I hope your ring didn't max out my card," he teased, and then laughed when she looked worried. "I'm just kidding."

"I shouldn't have chosen such an expensive ring."

He leaned over and kissed her, as if he had every right, and Caroline sighed in contentment. In her heart he did.

"Caroline, I'm not in your father's stratosphere as far as money goes, but most people consider me a wealthy man." He kissed her again. "In fact, now that I'm marrying you, I'd be considered very wealthy indeed."

Caroline smiled up at him, trying to hide the fact that his words disturbed her. They could so easily be interpreted the wrong way. Her father's claim about Max saying he's the father of her baby just to get to his money came back to haunt her.

"Is something wrong?"

"No! Nothing."

The waiter returned for Max to sign the bill. She watched him write in the tip with almost no pause. There was another difference between men and women.

Men seemed to know how much to tip without ever stopping to calculate. When she signed for— "Max!" She grabbed his arm as the waiter walked away.

"What is it, sweetheart? You want something more? A sudden urge for a pickle?"

She ignored his teasing. "Max! I may have found a way to prove Adrian wrong."

"How?"

"Charge cards! I must have charged something during those two weeks. If the charge was here in the Denver area, instead of Las Vegas, then we'll have our proof."

"Brilliant," Max agreed, kissing her again. Then he took her hand and pulled her from the booth. "Come on. Let's go check your records."

They sat in tense silence as Max drove to her house. Too much rested on the result of their search for any idle chitchat.

"Where do you keep your records?" Max asked as they came to a stop in front of her house.

"There's a desk in my bedroom. Let's start there. If we don't find anything, we'll ask Mrs. Lamb."

Fifteen minutes later, Caroline called down to the kitchen. When Mrs. Lamb reached her bedroom door, Caroline was waiting for her.

"Mrs. Lamb? Where else would I keep my records? My bills, my files."

"Why, right here, child. Oh, my stars, you two have made a mess. What are you looking for?"

"We're looking for either of my charge card bills," Caroline explained.

Mrs. Lamb looked puzzled but she moved over to the bed to peer at the pile of paper. "Why, here they are, dear, right here on top."

"No, Mrs. Lamb, those are my current bills. I'm looking for the bills from late June, when I went away."

Mrs. Lamb looked from Caroline to Max and back to Caroline, slowly shaking her head. "Once you pay them, dear, you throw them out."

Caroline sank down onto the bed, not noticing the papers under her. "Surely not," she gasped. "Don't I have to save them for—for taxes or something?"

"They don't allow interest deductions anymore, you know, and you don't have business expenses since you don't have a business. Why save them?"

Caroline closed her eyes, fighting to keep the tears from slipping out. So close. She'd thought they would find proof.

"Caroline," Max said softly, his arms coming around her as he pulled her up into his arms. "It's all right. We'll find another way."

"I'm sorry," Mrs. Lamb apologized.

"It's not your fault, Mrs. Lamb," Max assured her.

Caroline lifted her face from his chest. "Max is right, Mrs. Lamb. You've done all you could to help. Can I call them in the morning, Max? Could they tell me over the phone if I made any charges then?"

"Good idea, Caroline. I'm sure they can. You won't get actual documents to back you up for several days, but your father would listen to reason, wouldn't he?"

Mrs. Lamb and Caroline looked at each other and laughed. Suddenly Caroline felt better. "That's not a known trait for my father, but we'd convince him."

"Then maybe we still have hope," he said with a smile, kissing her forehead.

"Well, I'll just go back downstairs. You two probably want to be alone," Mrs. Lamb said, edging to the door.

"No, I have to leave," Max said, stepping back from Caroline. She looked at him in surprise.

"You do? Why?"

He looked at the bed before he looked at her. "You need to get a lot of rest tonight. And if I'm here, I don't think you will."

Caroline's cheeks burned a bright red. She knew exactly what he was thinking. And she liked it. But he was right. Tomorrow could be a difficult day.

"Then you walk him to the door, and I'll straighten up this mess. That way, you can get right to bed as soon as you come back upstairs," Mrs. Lamb suggested.

With a thanks sent the housekeeper's way, Max took Caroline's hand and pulled her from the room. After closing the door behind him, he wrapped his arms around her and kissed her.

"Oh, Max," she murmured, "maybe you should change your mind."

"I'd like to, but your father's house isn't the place. And tonight isn't the time. Tomorrow night we'll do our celebrating."

Caroline suddenly thought of the little boy whistling as he walked through the graveyard. She hoped Max's words weren't indicative of his fear that tomorrow night she'd be sharing her life with Adrian. A shudder seized her.

He pulled her tighter. "Something wrong?"

"No. I'm just missing you already."

Another kiss only made her want more.

"I have to go, Caroline," Max insisted, sounding desperate.

"You don't want to be with me?" she asked, surprised.

He gave her a bear hug. "Don't be ridiculous. I want to be with you too much. Now, walk me to the door," he insisted, tugging her toward the stairs.

They walked down arm in arm, not talking. Caroline was thinking about the next morning and how early she could call the credit card company. And how soon she'd see Max again.

The sound of the sun room door opening scarcely registered, but the voices that she heard shook her from her thoughts.

She started to say something to Max, but her father and Adrian came into view.

"Caroline! I didn't hear you come in," Adrian said, walking forward. He stopped when he got a good look at her and Max, their arms entwined.

"I really don't think your behavior is appropriate," he finally said.

"We've been over this subject before," Caroline said, keeping her arm around Max. "I don't believe your proof and I don't want to marry you."

"But you promised. It's my right as the father of your child."

Max turned loose of her and stepped down another step. "I'm tired of your statements like that, Meadows. You are not the father of this baby."

"I have proof."

"Yeah, and I'd like to see it. Just where is this proof?"

"I have it in safekeeping," Adrian assured him, but Caroline noted he took a step backward. Max moved forward again.

"At your apartment?"

"No. It's being repaired. Caroline ripped it. And that reminds me, Caroline, I came to take you to my apartment. As you requested."

His attempt to make her feel guilty didn't work. "Didn't Daddy tell you? I wanted to see it this morning, not this evening."

"I don't understand what a few hours' difference could make."

"Oh, I think you do. Otherwise, you would've told the man to let me in."

"Don't be ridiculous. I just didn't want you to see the place before it was cleaned."

"By the way, Adrian, where are we going on our honeymoon?" Caroline suddenly asked.

"Honeymoon?" he repeated, as if he'd never heard the word before.

"Nowhere with him," Max growled.

She grinned, loving the jealousy in his voice, but she looked at Adrian, waiting for a response.

"Well, I haven't—there's been no time—I thought we'd go to Vegas. Kind of retrace our steps," Adrian finished with a rush, looking quite proud of himself.

Caroline stared at Adrian, a memory suddenly filling her head. She turned slowly to look at her father. "Why didn't you say anything?"

"What are you talking about?" James demanded.

"I remembered something. I hate Las Vegas. You took me there when I turned twenty-one, remember, Daddy?" She turned to grin at Max. "I had a miserable trip. I vowed I'd never go back to Las Vegas."

"And your father knew that?" Max stared at James.

"So what? Love can change a person's mind. Besides, she's older, now. Her tastes have changed since she was twenty-one," James blustered.

"Not that much. So that's another reason why I don't believe your 'proof.'"

Adrian had that bland expression on his face that she hated. "You have other reasons?"

"Yes, I do."

"What are they?"

Caroline started to answer and then closed her mouth. "No, I don't think I'll tell you. I have no physical proof, but I may have by tomorrow. So I'll just wait. But I wouldn't be counting on marrying me tomorrow, Adrian."

"You're bluffing," he said, a tight smile on his face. "You made a promise and I'll expect you to keep it tomorrow evening."

"I will," she agreed, without smiling in return, "unless the private detective I've hired finds something interesting."

"Or maybe the one I've hired," Max added, standing behind Caroline, his hands on her shoulders.

Adrian stared at them, his mouth open, his cheeks paling. "You—you've hired a detective?" He spun around to face James. "How could you let them do that? Make them call them off!"

"Now, Adrian, don't worry about it. After all, you've got proof that you're telling the truth. And once you're married to my Caroline," James added, "you'll be a member of the family."

"It could be a very costly membership, Adrian," Caroline said, determined not to ignore her father's blatant bribery. "You'd better be sure it's worth the price."

Chapter Sixteen

Her wedding day.

Somehow, Caroline hadn't thought it would be like this—nausea, fear, worry. The bridal magazines didn't describe wedded bliss that way.

As soon as her stomach was settled, she got out of bed and quickly dressed. She wanted to call the credit card companies as soon as their offices opened.

She was pacing the floor when Mrs. Lamb knocked on the door with her breakfast trey.

"You're already up?" the housekeeper asked, noting that Caroline was dressed in shorts and a T-shirt.

"Yes. I'm waiting to call about my credit cards."

"You can eat breakfast while you wait. Your mother is already up, too. She has a long list of things for you to do. And your dress was just delivered. The alterations have been made, but you should try it on as soon as possible. Your mother wanted me to remind you that the rehearsal is at three." She paused to take a deep breath. "I think that's all at the moment, but presents continue to arrive, and I think I'm going crazy."

Caroline gave the woman a hug. "I know, Lambie, but it will all be over soon. You've been a real trouper about everything."

Mrs. Lamb returned the hug. "I'm going to miss you when you're gone, Caroline. Oh, my stars, I will."

The housekeeper hurried from the room, whether to hide tears or simply to tackle all the chores waiting for her, Caroline didn't know. But that simple remark brought home to Caroline suddenly how much her life was about to change. Whether she married Adrian or Max, she would no longer live at home with her parents. She would no longer be independent. She would be part of a pair.

An unhappy pair, if the other one was Adrian.

If it was Max, she would be thrilled, but... but there were still some difficulties to work out.

She automatically ate her breakfast, thinking about her future, about the child she was carrying, the man she would share that child with.

When eight o'clock came, she put the tray aside and reached for the phone. Though it took several minutes to be connected to the right department, she persisted until she found someone who could answer her question.

"No, Miss Adkins. For that two-week period, you made no charges. There is a charge about three days after the date you gave me, but not during those two weeks."

"Thank you."

She dialed the second number, and again, after some delays, received the same answer. Depression threatened, but Caroline was getting angry. That emotion

energized her as she paced the room. How had she paid
for those two weeks? Surely she hadn't relied on the
man, whichever one he was.

Her bank account!

She called the bank and asked for activities during
that two-week period.

"Why, no, Miss Adkins. Well, on the day before the
date you gave me, you made a substantial withdrawal.
Do you want that information?"

"Yes, please."

"You withdrew twenty-five hundred cash, here at the
bank. Does that help?"

"Yes, thank you." No, thank you. At least she knew
she had paid her own way, she thought, but it didn't tell
her where she had spent that money.

Her hand was still resting on the telephone when it
rang. She jumped as if she'd received an electrical
shock.

"Caroline?" Max asked, his voice eager. "Did you
call about your charges?"

"Yes. There were none."

After a painful silence, he simply said, "Oh."

"I know. I also called the bank. I withdrew a lot of
cash the day before I left."

"That fits with what the hotel guy told me."

"What? What did he tell you?"

"That you paid in cash."

"They have a record of it? I registered there? Of
course I did. Why didn't you tell me?" Hope filled her
as she waited for his response.

"Yes, you registered, but not under your own name.
I don't know why, since you told *me* your real name."

"Then how do you know it was me with the fake name?"

"Because I knew your room number. They only had one person stay for two weeks in that room during that time period. So I assumed it was you. But I can't prove it, and that's why I didn't say anything."

"What name did I use?"

"Leslie…uh, McBay, McKay, something like that."

"Leslie McVey?"

"Maybe. Does that name mean something to you?"

"Yes. That's Daddy's secretary's name."

"Well, it sure wasn't his secretary that I walked to the door and kissed good-night," Max assured her.

Caroline couldn't resist a chuckle at the picture of Max romancing the stiff and proper, elderly Miss McVey. She had been her father's secretary for more than twenty years.

"What's so funny?"

"Nothing, Max." Her amusement faded as she realized they still had nothing to show for all their hard work. "It's just—I'm getting scared, Max. What if we can't find any proof before—" She broke off, unable to voice the event scheduled for the evening.

"You could break your promise."

She almost chewed a hole in her bottom lip, trying to think of an answer to his statement.

"Forget I said that," he said gruffly. "That's frustration speaking. But Caroline, you're not going to live with this man, are you?"

"No. I'm only marrying him to—to give the baby its daddy's name," she assured him.

"Damn it, Caroline. I won't put up with you calling my baby his."

She covered her eyes, unable to face even the soothing blues of her bedroom. "Max, please. I'm sure my memory will come back soon. If—when I know the baby is yours, then we'll get married, okay?"

"And if you don't recover your memory?"

"I will! I know I will! It just may not happen before tonight." She drew a deep, shuddering breath and leaned back against her pillow. "Max?"

"Yeah?"

"Are you going to come to the wedding?"

Silence.

"I know I'm asking a lot, Max, but I'd like for you to be there."

"Of course I'll be there."

She knew those words cost him. But she needed him there in the church with her. She needed to be able to see him, to know that even if she had to marry Adrian, Max was there. And, according to him, would always be there.

"Thank you."

"No problem. I'll see you."

Caroline hung up the phone and slid back down onto the pillow, wrapping her arms around her and thinking about Max Daniels and the time they'd shared . . . that she could remember. How she wished he were here with her now, holding her, loving her. When Max held her in his arms, she believed nothing could go wrong.

She needed that confidence now.

Her mother knocked on her door. "Caroline? Are you awake? You need to get dressed," she added as she opened the door and found her daughter lying on the bed.

"What's the hurry? We're not having the rehearsal until three, are we?" Caroline asked, not moving.

"I guess I forgot to tell you that we're having a bridesmaid luncheon at noon. There's just so much to remember, it must've slipped my mind. And, of course, you have a hair and manicure appointment before that. They'll do touch-ups this evening, so you'll be perfect for the wedding. And then, you need to get started on your thank-you notes. After all, the sooner you do, the sooner you'll be finished. And, of course, to write your thank-you notes, you have to open your gifts. You'll receive a lot more this evening at the wedding. And—"

Since it seemed she had an unending list, Caroline interrupted. "Mother, I'll keep the hair and manicure appointment, but I thought Chelsea was going to be my only attendant, so what's the point of a bridesmaids' luncheon?"

"Dear, we couldn't have a proper wedding with just your sister as an attendant. Neiman's found four matching gowns and have expressed them here. And," Amelia paused, a triumphant air about her, "I found four of your friends who are the right size."

"I've heard of choosing bridesmaids for bizarre reasons, but it never occurred to me to choose them by dress size. Are you sure I know any of them?"

"Of course you do. There's Lilly, Ann, Sylvia..."

Caroline stopped listening. She didn't care who the attendants were. She just wanted the evening to be over, finished. And tomorrow morning she'd start divorce proceedings. She couldn't remain married to Adrian.

"Caroline? Are you listening?" Amelia demanded, apparently recognizing her daughter's distraction.

"I suppose," Caroline responded, suddenly feeling very tired.

"Well, come downstairs and we'll get started. It's already nine o'clock."

Nine o'clock. Only ten hours until the wedding.

MAX PUT DOWN THE PHONE and stared at the wall in front of him. What could he do now? The PI's secretary knew nothing. Well, almost nothing.

She'd said he had a line on the photographer. But the wedding was tonight. His heartbeat accelerated at the thought of Caroline meeting Adrian at the altar, taking the vows *he* wanted to share with her. She was his! His ring should be on her finger.

His arms should be around her. His lips should be caressing hers. His—if he didn't stop this kind of thinking, he'd have to take a cold shower.

But he wanted more than her body. He wanted to care for her, to share with her, to laugh with her. He wanted the right to be in her life.

"Max, a call on line two," Susan said through the intercom.

He snatched up the receiver, hoping it was Caroline or the detective he'd hired. Instead, it was a contractor working on one of his houses. And it was already eleven o'clock.

"YOU'RE NOT EATING anything," Amelia whispered to Caroline.

"I'm afraid if I do, it will come right back up," Caroline whispered in return.

Since they were in an elegant restaurant hastily hired for the bridesmaids' luncheon, throwing up would be highly inappropriate.

"Then don't try the eggplant," Amelia warned, and waved to the waiter hovering in the background. "My daughter would like some crackers, please."

She hadn't expected such understanding from her mother, but Amelia had tried to help her through the morning. Even Chelsea, now seated on her other side, had held her hand. But as the impending wedding drew closer, her stomach grew less reliable.

"Are you okay?" Chelsea whispered.

"I suppose," she answered as she had earlier that morning. "But I wish I could lie down for a while."

"As soon as we can get away, we'll take a taxi to my house," Chelsea said. "You can rest for an hour before the rehearsal. If you go home with Mother, there will be too much going on."

Caroline stared at her sister. "That's very sweet of you, Chelsea. I'd like that." She'd like even more to see Max, but at least, for just a little while, she would be out of the whirlwind that seemed to be consuming her. And she could use the telephone. To call the detective. And Max.

How she wished she could see him. Just a few minutes. To feel his arms around her. If she were preparing for a wedding with Max, things would be so different. She'd be feeling enthusiastic, not nauseous.

"Caroline," one of the bridesmaids called, "Tell us about your wedding gown. What's it like?"

Caroline went blank. She couldn't remember any of the details. Except that it was white, of course.

Amelia spoke, squeezing her daughter's hand beneath the tablecloth. "Oh, you'll just love it. The skirt is..."

Chelsea chipped in, describing Caroline's going-away suit, something else her mother had insisted she purchase, and she relaxed in her chair. Her mother and sister were taking care of her.

She surreptitiously checked her watch. Almost one o'clock.

She needed to talk to Max.

"HE'S NOT HERE, Caroline," Susan said cheerfully.

Caroline could have flung the telephone receiver across the room in frustration. "Do you know where he is?" she managed to say in civil tones.

"Nope. And, confidentially, he's been acting real strange today. All on edge, you know? But he left here about one o'clock, and he told me he wouldn't be back the rest of the day. That's unlike Max."

After ending the call, Caroline slumped against the pillow on Chelsea's guest bed. True to her word, Chelsea had gotten Caroline away from the luncheon to the relative quietness of her home. But Caroline had been unable to rest.

Instead, she'd increased her frustration by calling the security firm and then Max. And getting no response from either one. The wedding was in just a few hours.

"Caroline?" Chelsea poked her head around the door.

"Yes?"

"Daddy's downstairs to take us to the rehearsal. Are you ready?"

No. She wasn't ready. She would never be ready to practice marrying Adrian. *Max, where are you?*

"Caroline?" Chelsea said again, and Caroline heard the concern in her sister's voice.

Wearily she pushed herself up from the bed. "Yes, I'm ready, Chelsea. As ready as I'll ever be."

When the two of them came down the stairs, her father was waiting.

"Ah, the beautiful bride and the matron of honor," he boomed, a big smile on his face. "What a wonderful day."

Caroline had seen better.

"SHE ISN'T HERE?" Max asked Mrs. Lamb as she opened the door to him. "Do you know where she is?"

"Well, I guess she's at the rehearsal, Mr. Daniels. It's supposed to start at three, and it's almost that time now."

He'd forgotten about the rehearsal. Which wasn't surprising since he was going out of his head. The thought of Caroline belonging to another man was unbearable, even if it was in name only, for a short time. She was his. Why couldn't everyone understand that?

"Can you tell me how to find the church?" he finally asked. Mrs. Lamb's directions were clear and the church was nearby, so he wasted no time getting back into his truck. He didn't know what he would say to Caroline when he found her. He only knew he had to see her. Now.

The limo, with Lewis leaning against it, was parked in front of the church. Max left his pickup by the curb and stopped to ask if Caroline was inside.

"Yes, sir. They're having the rehearsal."

With a nod of thanks, he hurried through the double doors of the church. The shadows, after the bright sunlight, made it difficult to see for a moment. But he had no difficulty recognizing the voice that called his name.

"Max!" At least Caroline sounded happy to see him.

"What are you doing here?" her father demanded almost at once.

He ignored James Adkins, reaching Caroline as she hurried to him, taking her hands in his.

"I had to see you."

"I've been trying to call you," she assured him, her eyes devouring him in a way that set him on fire.

"Any word?"

"No, you?"

He reluctantly shook his head.

"Caroline, come over here and get ready for the rehearsal," her father insisted as he approached them.

"I don't mean to interrupt, Mr. Adkins," Max said politely, though he was feeling far from calm. "I just need to talk to Caroline for a minute or two."

"The—the groom isn't here yet, Daddy, so I have time to talk to Max," Caroline assured her father.

James Adkins couldn't argue with that, Max realized, but he seemed determined to stand beside them.

"Alone, Daddy," Caroline insisted.

Max was grateful she was the one to tell her father to go away. He was trying not to alienate Caroline's family any more than necessary. But the five steps James Adkins took didn't exactly give them a lot of privacy. Not when Max wanted to pull her into his arms.

"I'm sorry, Max, but I don't know where we could be alone," Caroline whispered.

"You must know I want to kiss you," he said with a rueful smile.

She smiled in return but shook her head no. "I just know I want you to kiss me. I want to feel your arms around me."

"Caroline," he protested. "Don't tempt me." He squeezed her hands, the most intimacy he could manage with a dozen people watching them. "Who are all these people?"

She looked over her shoulder, as if she'd forgotten their audience. "Mother rounded up some bridesmaids. Then there's the florist, and Daddy, and...I don't know who else. They don't matter. Did you call your detective?"

"Yeah. Several times. The secretary recognizes my voice now. Damn but you're beautiful." His gaze traced her hair as the curls tickled her brow, then moved on to her full lips. Hunger to touch her filled his gut and he had to fight to keep his distance.

"Max, I want *you* to be the groom!" she wailed softly, pain in her eyes.

"I want that, too. And if you say the word, I'll tell your father right now." He watched as tears filled her eyes. He knew what her answer would be. She felt obligated to keep her word, to offer the only man with proof the opportunity to give his name to her baby. But it was too high a price. And he was having to pay, as well as Caroline.

"I can't, Max. I can't."

One tear escaped and trailed down her beautiful face. He released one of her hands to gently wipe it away. The desire to pull her into his arms, to comfort, to love, was almost overwhelming. But he couldn't.

"Don't cry, sweetheart. Do what you have to do, and we'll work it out." It cost him a lot to offer such reassurance, but he loved her. He couldn't add to her difficulties.

She closed her eyes and then stared at him again, a brilliance in them that almost shattered his control. "I love you, Max Daniels."

"Damn, Caroline, you have to wait and tell me that now? With an audience, just before you marry someone else?" he demanded. "You must have a lot in common with the Marquis de Sade."

She gave him a watery chuckle that only made him want her more. "I just thought I should mention it."

"Thanks," he said dryly as he lifted her hands to his lips. Hand kissing should be all right, even if she was about to marry another man.

Wrong. The touch of her skin only made him want to continue right up those arms to her neck, her lips, her— he groaned as she licked her bottom lip.

"Caroline! Don't do that!"

She jumped and blinked rapidly. "Don't do what?"

"Don't lick your lips."

"But they were dry," she said, a puzzled look on her face.

"Sweetheart, I'm having a hard enough time keeping my distance without you making me think about—"

"Ah, this must be the lovely bride," an elderly man said, walking up to them. "I can always tell. They all look positively beaming with love. And that look in their eyes." The minister turned to Max. "And this, I presume, is the lucky groom."

Chapter Seventeen

"I have never been so embarrassed in my life," James Adkins said again, pacing about the bride's room.

"Daddy, you've told us that at least a hundred times since the rehearsal," Chelsea reminded him as she repositioned Caroline's veil.

"And I still don't think that's the truth," Amelia added. "I think you were even more embarrassed that time you lost your wallet and couldn't pay the bill at that restaurant in Philadelphia."

"Amelia, that's not the point!" he exclaimed, his irritation rising.

"Then what is the point, Daddy?" Caroline asked. She was hanging on to her patience by a thread, but she didn't know how much longer she could do so.

"The point is you shouldn't have been making goo-goo eyes with another man!"

"Goo-goo eyes?" exclaimed all three women at the same time.

"Well, whatever they call it these days. You know what I mean."

Caroline drew a deep breath and then turned to her mother and sister. "I need to talk to Daddy alone." She had rediscovered a kinship with her mother and sister that meant a great deal to her. But she had to face her father without their support.

When they were alone, she turned around to face him squarely, tugging the long satin train of her gown out of the way. "Daddy, you know I don't love Adrian. I'm not going to pretend I do."

"He's a good man, Caro. I wouldn't let you marry someone who would hurt you, but you're not giving him a chance. You keep hanging on to that other man, the one you're infatuated with."

"I'm not infatuated with Max, Daddy. I love him. And he loves me."

"Then why are you marrying Adrian? That's not fair to him."

She clenched her teeth in frustration. "I'm marrying Adrian because I promised you, and because he offered proof that he's the father of my baby. But I don't love him."

"But, Caroline, it's only fair that you marry him. After all, you've admitted that's his baby."

"No, I haven't. I said he offered proof. I don't know what to think. I want this baby to be Max's, Daddy. But—but I can't be sure. And I promised you."

"Baby," James began, calling her his pet name that he hadn't used in several years, "I only want what's best for you. Adrian is a good man."

"Caroline," Chelsea said, sticking her head into the room. "It's time. The wedding is starting."

With a sinking in the pit of her stomach, Caroline turned and looked in the mirror one more time. She would give anything to know that Max was waiting for her at the end of that aisle.

But he wasn't.

She hadn't seen him since that embarrassing scene in the vestibule. But he'd promised he'd be here. Had he arrived? Was he sitting in the church, waiting to watch her marry another man?

Why hadn't they found something to prevent this disaster from taking place? Why hadn't they found proof that Adrian was lying? He had to be lying.

But it was too late.

Her father cleared his throat. "Ready, Caroline?"

No, she wasn't ready. But it seemed she had no choice.

Standing, she lifted her veil to cover her face. Her father hurriedly assisted her and then opened the door, waiting for her to precede him.

The bridesmaids had begun marching solemnly down the aisle. Chelsea, the last to go down, was waiting her turn and gave Caroline an encouraging smile.

She tried to smile back. She really did. But she couldn't. This should have been the happiest moment of her life. Instead, it was the worst.

Her father extended his arm and she placed her hand through it. The music changed, rising in sound, emphasizing the moment. They stepped through the double doors and began the long walk down the aisle.

But instead of looking at her groom, the bride was searching the audience, looking for a certain dark-haired, blue-eyed man who owned her heart.

As her gaze scanned those seated along the aisle, she saw a young woman she thought she should've recognized. Something was familiar about her, but Caroline couldn't think what it could be.

Then her gaze connected with Max's, and she forgot everything else. Max. The man she loved with all her heart. The man she wasn't marrying.

SHE WAS BEAUTIFUL. The most beautiful bride in the world, Max decided. But she wasn't his.

Since he'd left her at the church that afternoon, Max had paced various floors. He'd made every phone call he could think of to try to prevent what was about to happen. He had prayed a few prayers, hoping for divine intervention. He didn't know what else to do.

Except watch the only woman he'd ever loved marry another man.

Along with half of Denver. The church was full, which was amazing considering the short notice. Not that he cared. He would've married Caroline anywhere. In fact, he might prefer a deserted island, so there would be no one to interfere with his plans for after the wedding.

He forced his thoughts away from holding Caroline and watched with real pain as her father transferred her hand from his arm to Adrian's.

"Dearly beloved..."

She was his dearly beloved, more than he'd ever realized was possible. He wanted her with every ounce of his body. But he wanted, needed more. He needed her heart, her head, her soul. He wanted to protect her, to care for her, to love her for the rest of his life. In sickness or in health.

He'd already proven the sickness bit. A smile played across his lips as he remembered holding her as she threw up. She'd looked as beautiful then as she did now, in her white satin. She would look as beautiful nine months pregnant, her stomach swollen with their child, as she did now, all slim and curvaceous.

She was his, he promised himself, and always would be. No matter what words were spoken here today.

SHE FELT HIS GAZE ON HER. It warmed her and yet made her pain all the greater. She loved one man and was marrying another.

Sneaking a peek at her groom from under her lashes, Caroline thought he was the most repulsive man in the world. Others might think him handsome with his blond good looks, but she only saw the greed she thought motivated him. He wanted her father's empire. And he would do whatever it took to reach his goal.

Even marry her.

So why was she helping him?

She'd told herself she was being honorable, giving her child its due. But she'd always promised herself she wouldn't marry a man who wanted her father's money. Pain surged through her head at the thought. Pain and memory.

"IF THERE IS ANY REASON this man and this woman should not be joined in holy matrimony, please speak now or forever hold your peace," the Reverend Mr. Spencer intoned, a beaming smile on his face.

"Stop!" Caroline exclaimed hoarsely.

"Stop!" Max exclaimed, rising from the pew, to the amazement of those around him.

"Stop!" exclaimed two men standing by the double doors at the back of the church.

The guests gasped in unison before an excited buzz spread across the audience. The minister, shock on his face, stared at each of those who had responded to his question. "My, this is most unusual."

"Just ignore them," Adrian said through clenched teeth. "Get on with the ceremony."

"Sir, you may not have noticed, but one of those who spoke was your bride," the cleric gently informed Adrian. "In good conscience, I cannot continue if the bride is unwilling."

"What's going on here?" James demanded, having left his seat beside Amelia and stepped to the altar.

"Mr. Adkins, there have been three objections to the wedding proceeding," the cleric explained. "I'm not sure what we should do, but I don't think the wedding should continue without discovering the reason for these interruptions."

"Caroline?" James demanded.

"I can't marry him, Daddy," she said, tears in her eyes. "He's not the father of my baby."

"You don't have proof of that," Adrian reminded her harshly.

"We do," a quiet voice said just behind him.

James, Caroline and Adrian turned around to face the strangers who had spoken last. At least they were strangers to Adrian, Caroline supposed. She knew one of them, the investigator she'd hired, and she was sure her father also knew him.

Just behind them stood Max. The man she loved, the man she'd hoped to marry. And the man she would have to walk away from.

And past Max, Caroline saw the entire church whispering, craning their necks, enjoying the show. They'd never seen a wedding like this one. And she hoped they never did again.

"I think it might be best if we retired to my office for a few minutes and sorted things out," the Reverend Mr. Spencer said.

James Adkins, his face growing redder by the minute, nodded in agreement. "All right." He turned to the audience. "There's a little confusion. If you'll just be patient, we'll resume the wedding shortly."

Caroline stared at her bouquet. She was afraid her father was promising more than he could deliver.

THE REVEREND Mr. Spencer's office was a large one, but it seemed small after everyone crowded in. In addition to the bride and groom, the pastor and the two detectives, James Adkins was joined by his wife and his younger daughter. And, of course, Max.

Caroline had taken one look at his determined face and turned away. Tears threatened and she didn't want to cry in front of any of them. Most especially Max.

"Now, I think we would all like to hear an explanation of what evidence you are talking about," Reverend Spencer said to the two men.

"Sir, we were hired by the bride and Mr. Daniels to determine if the picture this man showed them was valid. We have proof that it was not, and that he altered the picture to persuade Miss Adkins to marry him because he had gambling debts he couldn't pay."

As his audience stared at him, openmouthed, the man speaking, from James's security firm, extended his hand with a picture in it.

Even though Caroline no longer needed proof, she took the picture and stared at it. The woman in the church. It wasn't her face that was familiar. It was the tobacco brown coatdress, its lapels outlined in black, that was familiar. The dress in the picture. But in this photo, the head above the dress wasn't Caroline's. It was that young lady's.

"Who is she?"

"His secretary," Don Knowles said, stepping forward. "I'm sorry we didn't arrive before the wedding, but my flight was late."

"Mary?" James questioned, staring at his right-hand man. "You took Mary to Las Vegas?"

"There's more, Mr. Adkins," Joe Perkins said quietly. "But I think I should tell you in private."

James swiveled around to face Adrian again, his eyes narrowed, his jaw firm. The man stood frozen with fear on his pale face. James looked back at Perkins. "Okay. We'll talk after the wedding."

"There's still going to be a wedding?" the minister asked.

This time James turned to look at his daughter. "Yes, there's still going to be a wedding. I release you from your promise, Caroline. You can marry Max, as you wanted."

"Thank you, Mr. Adkins," Max acknowledged even as he moved toward Caroline.

"No!"

All eyes centered on her. At least her protest had stopped Max in his tracks. If he touched her, she wasn't sure she'd be able to continue.

"No, what? Caroline, this is what you wanted," James said.

"Yes, Caro, you said you wanted to marry Max," Chelsea added.

"I've changed my mind. I can't marry Max."

Her words were almost as astonishing as the interruptions in the church. Perhaps even more so to Max. James stepped closer to his daughter.

"Caro, it's okay. I want you to marry this man. He loves you. And since Adrian isn't the father of your baby, Max must be. I want my grandchild born on the right side of the blanket, remember?" When she didn't respond, he added, "And I want you to be happy."

She swallowed back tears. "Thank you, Daddy, but I can't marry Max."

"I think Caroline and I need some privacy to settle things," Max said quietly, sending a look to James, asking his cooperation.

"Yes, of course," James agreed, and began urging the others back into the sanctuary. There was pause as they encountered the eager stares of the audience, waiting for the next event in this singularly unusual wedding. Then James stepped forward and asked their patience, assuring them matters would be resolved very soon.

Caroline knew he was right. Only there wouldn't be a wedding. There couldn't be a wedding.

As the door closed behind the last of them, Max stepped toward her, and she backed away.

"Caroline, what's wrong? Why are you refusing to marry me?"

She looked at his beloved face and then turned away. It was too painful. How could she refuse when she loved him so much?

"Caroline?"

With her back to him, she said, "My memory returned."

"What? When? What do you remember? I'm the father, aren't I?"

She nodded her head.

The eager happiness she'd heard in his voice wasn't there when he asked his next question. "So what else do you remember? What is it that makes you say you won't marry me?"

Gathering her courage, she turned to face him. "I remember why I ran away."

There was no acknowledgment in his eyes, no shame, no guilt. He still didn't know what had gone wrong. But there was a question there. He wanted to know.

"I woke up and you weren't there. I had pulled on your T-shirt and started downstairs when I realized you had company."

"It was Jim, my foreman," he agreed, still looking puzzled.

"Yes. He was reminding you of the need for more financing, for an influx of capital."

Max frowned. "I remember. So? Are you refusing to marry me because you're afraid I can't support you?" His incredulity was irritating.

"I'm not the one who's in the wrong here!" she snapped. "You're the one who's marrying me for my money. Or I should say my father's money!"

"What?" Max exclaimed in a roar that was probably heard in the sanctuary, adding to the audience's enjoyment. "You accuse me of marrying you for your money just because my foreman and I were discussing my company's finances?"

The tears drew closer. She loved this man so much. "No, that's not why. He—he said you should just get a loan from me because I was probably kin to James Adkins, and then you wouldn't have any troubles." She watched as memory came back to him. "And you agreed, saying that had been your plan all along."

She turned away, unable to face the guilt that she knew would be on his face. He'd been her knight in shining armor, her one true love. Now that he knew she knew, he'd probably slink out the door, and she'd never see him again. Tears rolled down her cheeks.

"Caroline Adkins!" Max exclaimed as he spun her around to face him. "I ought to wring your neck!"

She stared at him in shock.

"That was a joke! I didn't know who you were!"

A sob broke from her before she said, "Of course you would say that."

"I not only say it, I have proof," he insisted, "And I can't believe you ran away without even asking me about it. We've wasted two months we could've shared."

"Max, I understand, but I can't marry you. It's okay, I forgive you." She thought she was being magnanimous. He didn't seem to feel the same way.

"Wringing your neck is too nice! I'm going bury you in a nest of fire ants," he threatened, and pulled her against him, wrapping his arms around her.

"Max!" she protested, "I'm not going to change my mind. The reason I was there, with you, was because I'd had an argument with my father. He said no one would ever marry me without wanting his money. I intended to prove him wrong." More tears fell as she finished. "Instead, I proved him right."

Max pressed her head against his shoulder. "Don't cry, sweetheart, or you'll have red eyes for our wedding. Listen to me, you crazy woman. I love you! I don't care how much money your father has. It has nothing to do with us. I had made a loan at the bank the day before, and I have the papers dated to prove it. If you'd hung around a little longer, you would've heard me explain that to Jim."

"The day before?" she asked, looking at him, hope in her gaze.

"Don't you remember? You wanted to go on another picnic and I had to cut it short? That was my appointment with the bank."

"And you have papers dated that day?"

"Sure do. I can even go home and get them, but that means the wedding will last a little longer than planned."

He brought his lips to hers in a kiss that shook her to her very toes. Max loved her.

"It's your call, Caroline. What are we going to do now?" he asked huskily.

She raised her hand to caress his cheek and then draw his lips to hers again. When she finally, reluctantly, pulled away, she whispered, "I think we should get married. After all, we have to think about *our* baby."

Max didn't hesitate. He scooped her up into his arms and carried her into the sanctuary, to everyone's surprise. Setting her down in front of the pastor, he said, "We'd like to be married, please."

And they were.

Epilogue

Six months later Caroline wasn't feeling quite as exuberant. Her body was heavy and her patience frazzled. Twins. He'd warned her. But somehow, when the doctor had confirmed Max's prediction four months ago, she hadn't realized just how big she would get.

"I'm the size of the Goodyear blimp," she muttered as she tried to find a comfortable position on the sofa. Not that Max seemed to notice. His loving care was the only thing that was getting her through these last days.

The doctor had said the babies might come early. She wanted them healthy. But she also wanted—ah! Caroline held her breath, stunned by the pain she'd just felt. What was that? Surely it couldn't be—

She grabbed the phone and called her doctor. His orders were succinct and firm. She pressed the speed dial for Max's beeper. The phone rang only seconds after she hung up.

"Caroline?"

"It's time, Max."

He didn't even answer, just hung up the phone. In spite of the anxiety she was feeling, Caroline chuckled.

The only person more worried than she about the birth was Max. He'd hovered over her so much, even she had protested.

Chelsea had assured her birth wasn't so bad. At least, that's what she'd said last week. Immediately after giving birth to her pretty baby girl, whom she'd named Amelia Lynn, she hadn't been quite as sure.

Another pain struck her about six minutes later, and Caroline was glad she'd called the doctor. The sound of the front door slamming told her Max had arrived.

"Sweetheart! Where are you?" he demanded even as he ran to the back of the house.

"In here," she said, pushing herself up from the sofa. "Get the suitcase from upstairs, please."

He raced up the stairs and back down before she was able to stand, arriving at her side to pull her up. Before she could take a step, he carefully lifted her into his arms and headed to the front door.

"Remember when you carried me into the church?" she whispered, giggling.

"How could I forget it with so many people watching us? By that time, I don't know what they expected."

He got her into the front seat of his truck and then kissed her quickly before shutting the door and hurrying to his side. "Put on your seat belt," he warned as he started the motor. "I don't intend for my babies to be born in a truck. I'd never hear the end of it from your father."

Caroline laughed again. Her father and Max had developed a fine relationship, as long as James didn't try to tell Max how to run his business. Her father finally had the son he'd so desperately wanted. One just as stubborn as him.

"Did you call your parents?" he asked.

"Not yet."

Max picked up the phone in his truck and pressed a button. "Miss McVey? Tell James it's time. We'll meet them at the hospital."

"Where it all began," Caroline murmured, and closed her eyes.

"BOYS! TWIN BOYS! Can you believe it?" James patted Max on the back.

"How's Caroline?" Amelia asked anxiously.

"Pretty tired, but happy."

Chelsea and Roddy rushed into the waiting room, their baby daughter in Roddy's arms. He'd blossomed as a father, amusing everyone with his newfound authority.

"She had twin boys!" James exclaimed, a beaming smile on his face.

"Is Caroline all right?" Chelsea asked.

"She's fine."

"Well, congratulations. Of course, I think girls are sweeter, but I'm sure your boys will be just fine."

"I couldn't agree with you more, Chelsea. Girls are definitely sweeter." He winked at Roddy. "At least I hope so," Max added, a big grin on his face. "I'm going back inside with Caroline. The babies will be taken up to the nursery if you want to see them."

"Are they big enough?" Amelia asked.

Max smiled. Caroline had thought they were too big. "They both weigh more than five pounds, so they'll be able to go home with us when it's time."

When he stepped back into the comparative quiet of the delivery room, Caroline lay with her eyes closed. He bent over to kiss her cheek.

"Hi," she murmured sleepily. "Did you tell them?"

"Yeah. Your dad's jumping for joy."

She opened one eye. "And you?"

"Thrilled to pieces," he assured her with a grin. "But I think you should know Chelsea and I agree that girls are sweeter."

She studied him, a puzzled look on her face. "You're not happy we had boys?"

"Of course I am. I just don't want Chelsea to feel superior to us. Next time, we'll have a girl."

"Next time?"

He grinned at the note of exasperation in her voice. She'd been terrific in the delivery room and as much as he wanted a little girl, he wasn't sure he'd want her to go through labor again. "We'll discuss it later," he whispered before kissing her.

Caroline slid her arms around his neck. Maybe they'd have a little girl. After a while. Max could convince her to do almost anything.

And next time, she thought, she'd need no convincing about who's the daddy.

Once in a while, there's a man so special, a story so different,
that your pulse races, your blood rushes. We call this

Trevor d'Laine is one such man, and LOVE BITES is one
such book.

Kay Erickson didn't believe in vampires, until this one skateboarded
into her life and swept her off her feet. Their love was star-crossed,
but held the promise of centuries of passion—if only one of them
would relinquish what they loved best....

Harlequin American Romance #582

LOVE BITES
by
Margaret St. George

Don't miss this exceptional, sexy hero. He'll make your
HEARTBEAT.

Available in May wherever Harlequin Books are sold.
Watch out for more Heartbeat stories, coming your way soon.

MILLION DOLLAR SWEEPSTAKES (III)

No purchase necessary. To enter, follow the directions published. Method of entry may vary. For eligibility, entries must be received no later than March 31, 1996. No liability is assumed for printing errors, lost, late or misdirected entries. Odds of winning are determined by the number of eligible entries distributed and received. Prizewinners will be determined no later than June 30, 1996.

Sweepstakes open to residents of the U.S. (except Puerto Rico), Canada, Europe and Taiwan who are 18 years of age or older. All applicable laws and regulations apply. Sweepstakes offer void wherever prohibited by law. Values of all prizes are in U.S. currency. This sweepstakes is presented by Torstar Corp., its subsidiaries and affiliates, in conjunction with book, merchandise and/or product offerings. For a copy of the Official Rules send a self-addressed, stamped envelope (WA residents need not affix return postage) to: MILLION DOLLAR SWEEPSTAKES (III) Rules, P.O. Box 4573, Blair, NE 68009, USA.

EXTRA BONUS PRIZE DRAWING

No purchase necessary. The Extra Bonus Prize will be awarded in a random drawing to be conducted no later than 5/30/96 from among all entries received. To qualify, entries must be received by 3/31/96 and comply with published directions. Drawing open to residents of the U.S. (except Puerto Rico), Canada, Europe and Taiwan who are 18 years of age or older. All applicable laws and regulations apply; offer void wherever prohibited by law. Odds of winning are dependent upon number of eligibile entries received. Prize is valued in U.S. currency. The offer is presented by Torstar Corp., its subsidiaries and affiliates in conjunction with book, merchandise and/or product offering. For a copy of the Official Rules governing this sweepstakes, send a self-addressed, stamped envelope (WA residents need not affix return postage) to: Extra Bonus Prize Drawing Rules, P.O. Box 4590, Blair, NE 68009, USA.

SWP-H395

With the advent of spring, American Romance is pleased to be presenting three exciting couples, each with their own unique reasons for needing a new beginning...for needing to enter into a marriage of convenience.

Meet the reluctant newlyweds in:

#580 MARRIAGE INCORPORATED
Debbi Rawlins
April 1995

#583 THE RUNAWAY BRIDE
Jacqueline Diamond
May 1995

#587 A SHOTGUN WEDDING
Cathy Gillen Thacker
June 1995

Find out why some couples marry first...and learn to love later. Watch for the upcoming "In Name Only" promotion.

IS BRINGING YOU A BABY BOOM!

NEW ARRIVALS

We're expecting! This spring, from March through May, three very special Harlequin American Romance authors invite you to read about three equally special heroines—all of whom are on a nine-month adventure! We expect each soon-to-be mom will find the man of her dreams—and a daddy in the bargain!

In March we brought you #576 BABY MAKES NINE by Vivian Leiber, and in April #579 WHO'S THE DADDY by Judy Christenberry. Now meet the expectant mom in:

#584 BABY BY CHANCE
by Elda Minger
May 1995

Look for the New Arrivals logo—and please help us welcome our new arrivals!

HARLEQUIN®

PRESENTS
RELUCTANT BRIDEGROOMS

Two beautiful brides, two unforgettable romances...
two men running for their lives....

My Lady Love, by Paula Marshall, introduces
Charles, Viscount Halstead, who lost his memory
and found himself employed as a stableboy by the
untouchable Nell Tallboys, Countess Malplaquet.
But Nell didn't consider Charles untouchable—
not at all!

Darling Amazon, by Sylvia Andrew, is the story of
a spurious engagement between Julia Marchant
and Hugo, marquess of Rostherne—an engagement
that gets out of hand and just may lead Hugo to
the altar after all!

Enjoy two madcap Regency weddings this May,
wherever Harlequin books are sold.

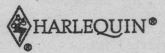